Fata Morgana

Fah'tuh Mor-gah'nah

BEU ORIELS

Ordering Information:

Prime Seven Media
518 Landmann St.
Tomah City, WI 54660
Printed in the United States of America

TABLE OF CONTENTS

PROLOGUE

I look...... I can't touch
I think.......I can't speak
Those yet, such beautiful words
Taciturn, tho'felt so strong
I don't dare to whisper.
He gives and I take
This haunting, lovely music
The sweet dynamo that ignites
A fire that burns so low
So soothing and ardent!
Something to be treasured
Intangible, like a shooting star
A mirage so mysterious
No fantasy could make reality!

Bound by strong chains
Chains of the past
Entangled like a web
Impossible to unravel
This current it flows

It excites, entices, unsettles

The oh, so very dangerous

Sacred ground, we dare

Not to tread, unless with

A finesse, lest we disturb

And destroy, these moments

So delightful, to be treasured

A Mirage so mysterious

No fantasy could make reality!

CHAPTER 1

THE MIRAGE

*L*ove is the most beautiful thing. It delights, sends a tingle that creeps through one's whole body and makes one giddy with happiness. It drives one so crazy that it's often difficult to distinguish reality from truth. Those glowing feelings filled and exhilarated Melani as she kept reminiscing. A great happiness filled and spread through her. Those few moments together! This couldn't be happening to her. She was happily married. She loved her husband and her two lovely children Pete and Kodi. They had been married for fifteen years

Born in Etobicoke - Ontario in the year 1952. Melani, was the youngest of five children. Slim but petite. Everything about her was dramatic, her dark sparkling eyes, her coal-black hair, even the way her eyes misted when she felt romantic. Her rich dark hair curled around her heart-shaped face.

As the years went by she surprised herself by once again falling in love!

"Is it possible to love two people at the same time? Would it be possible for me to set free the ties that bind?"

These questions went through her mind as she got into a pensative mood.

Giovani was born in Genova, Italy. He was six foot, five on the slim side, short wavy brown hair and brown eyes which had a tint of gold when he smiled. He was a very possessive person. Unknown to Melani, the negative influences of the past had left an indelible mark on his life.

Outwardly, it seemed as if Melani intentionally drew the attention of men to her. But it didn't take him long to discover that she had a long list of girl-friends too. There was no age limit. She had that enormous magnetism that must have left a number of broken hearts behind her wherever she went. This courted envy, hatred and sometimes even surprised her husband on various occasions that he would often revert to spurts of jealousy, beyond control, which he soon grew out of it as time went by.

But on the contrary she loved her husband. Strong as always she patiently faced the numerous contradictions of life. To her, her greatest priority had always been her family and that superceded all other feelings, which at times difficult to control would have made anyone sway and join the category of a fallen angel.

But she thought to herself, "It must be hard to have to live with a person like me. I am just so different, quite a heady cocktail, that could drive anybody crazy. We are two characters maybe complimentary but at the same time, quite the contrary."

CHAPTER 2

THE FAMILY OUTING

They had just arrived in Oakville - a very beautiful lakeside city. They drove around admiring the beauty of the place.

Down town was simple with mostly low buildings except for a couple of tall buildings, which represented commercial centres. There were many little boutiques, instead of the big department stores or malls, which in a way spelt exclusive! Most of these little shops looked very similar to those in Europe.

The surrounding area was beautiful Here most of the people lived in pretty medium-sized detached homes. Most of them along the waterfront. There were also some great big homes surrounded by lovely gardens and terraces overlooking the lake.

Along-side the lakefront, some boats with very colourful sails and a couple of the most expensive yachts lay anchored. Numerous boys and couples sat along the pier holding on to their fishing rods.

"Have you been lucky, today sir?" Pete interrupted Jerry who was very engrossed in fishing.

"Oh, hi Pete! What brings you to this part of the world?"

"Just this very special day out with the family. It's my birthday"! He said, "I'm a grow –up man, sweet sixteen. I can actually start driving now. How do like that?"He answered, with a smirk on his face, hoping to make his friend feel envious.

He used to be one of the most presumptious guys in school, when he was in Burnhamthorpe High School, a year ago before his parents moved. Often be bullied the weaker boys and even tried it on Pete on one occasion, when they nearly got into a fight, but ended peacefully.

"Oh, happy birthday to you, enjoy yourself. And where's the birthday cake?" He teased.

"Well that's no problem. Do you think I can drag you away from here!" answered Pete. They broke into splits realizing, that, that was not going to occur.

"Regarding the fish, of course we do! We always catch many, but most of the times we throw them back into the lake. You see most of us here, enjoy fishing but we'd rather put the fish back into the lake. Our priority is to keep them in their own environment, instead of our pots." He answered graciously, as he looked on impressed by Pete's parents who were elegantly dressed. They waved goodbye.

They continued their walk along the shore where the numerous geese very typical of this area were busy chasing each other, or trying to draw the attention of their partners. Others - spreading their wings began to flutter them and then slowly glided along the water, each time picking up speed and finally, splashing water around them as they smoothly lifted their bodies in flight, swooping up, into the sky, to fly away. Others would of and on interrupt their smooth swim as they suddenly ducked into the water, looking for food, always coming up with a prize in their beaks.

The Fellini children really enjoyed the times they went out with their parents. In Spring and Autumn they often went mushroom – picking. They all enjoyed staying outdoors whenever possible. They seemed to be a very happy family and got on well with each other.

"This would be a great place to come if you have any problems to solve. It helps one to see and understand things clearly and put them in their right perspective!" These were Linda's words, trying to convince her to move to Oakville.

CHAPTER 3

THE RUMBLE

It was half past twelve now, and Pete had more practical things to concern himself.

"I don't know about the rest of you, but I am starving! Can you hear my tummy rumbling?

He places his mum's hand over his tummy. Dad, look, there are many restaurants around. Don't they look great?" Many people seemed to feel the same and it looked as if all of them would soon fill up.

Melani fought off the all-pervading drowsiness that she felt as the lapping of the water had such a calming effect on the brain. This was her usual time for a nap.

No sooner than she stood up, the children fastened their pace as they started the hunt for a place to eat.

"I can see many popular restaurants. Don't they all look inviting? But look at all those classy restaurants where only the upper class patrons seemed to enjoy dining. Their stream-lined cars parked around that area clearly shows that they could afford all kinds of Gourmet food that must be offered inside.

Part of the menu that's posted outside said, "Fresh Lobsters and Crabs – the specialty of today! And all kinds of delicacy. There were many waiting to be shown inside.

"No, let's go somewhere, where they won't keep us waiting." Pete pleaded.

Luckily they didn't have to search long. They went to the Keg their favourite spot where the atmosphere matched the cuisine as well.

"Deference is a quality I lack and here it isn't required," said Pete.

They didn't have to wait long to be served either. They were shown to a cosy little area near a very unusual fire-place.

"Fourteenth century wood-work," commented the Maitre when she observed Kodi examining it carefully. It had all kinds of figures around it. The kids dropped all pretense of perfect behaviour and ignored the menu card, offered to them. They knew what they wanted.

"Tacos" for me - Mexican food - but in fact it had two enormous hamburghers with all the toppings and trimmings, surrounded indeed, by crisp golden tacos smothered with melting cheese. It didn't take Pete long to wolf down all that was in his plate. His sister who was quite happy to follow suit, wasn't far behind. What Mom and Dad had ordered didn't escape Pete.

Giovani had a very thick medium - raw, rump steak, with baked potatoes. They were wrapped in aluminum foil. Once opened one could see the steam rise from it.

"Doesn't that look yummy, yummy, and that cream cheese! It surely looked delectable! Dad can I get some, too?" said Pete.

"Can I have some, too?" he said swallowing the last mouthful of cucumber, lettuce and tomato.

But he stopped himself when his dad said, "So does that mean we can save on the dessert?"

"Oh no, I completely forgot about that… no… I'll skip that for now." He said with a laugh The family joined in.

"I'll have ice-cream with crunchy sugared walnuts!" Said Kodi.

Gio had just a black coffee, while Melani ordered some strawberries with cream.

They paid the bill and were back to the lakeshore.

"A walk would do everyone good, after that enormous meal, don't you think," he asked turning to look at the rest of the family.

So they continued walking enjoying the bracing fresh air. Melani and the children were so taken up with the place that she suggested on checking on house prices. This was a great excuse for seeing Linsay, one of her best friends.

Melani and the children were so taken up with the place that she suggested on checking on house prices. This was a great excuse for seeing Linsay, one of her best friends.

"A walk is just what we need now, after stuffing ourselves like that!" Giovanni said blithely.

CHAPTER 4

MELANI CALLS FRIEND

*I*t didn't long before, "Eh, look at this, house for sale!" Both the kids chimed in together. "Why don't we check on house prices?" Suggested Melani. "This is a great excuse for me to visit one of my good friends, Lindsay."

"You wouldn't want to disappoint Mum, do you, dad? She hardly ever goes any where, please dad. Why can't we?" He tried to persuade his father, knowing that he is more of a hermit. Besides his routine morning coffee at a habitual restaurant, he never went anywhere. Melani was not one for cafés. She enjoyed doing her regular exercises at the gym, besides swimming. And of course attending to the daily chores of the house.

CHAPTER 5

OAKVILLE

Oakville is reckoned to be one of the most exclusive areas in Ontario. Its golf courses had hosted World Championships. It's peaceful environment. It has five drive-in movie theatres, exclusive restaurants – quaint though lively the downtown area has high end boutiques, numerous Café's and pastry shops. Blackforest pastry shop is a unique place to visit with all its mouth-watering specialties.

The scenery was delightful. The city is built along the water-front. It took Gio no more persuading to fall in with Melani's proposal.

This was a great excuse for Melani to contact one of her very close friends. A couple of minutes later she was on the phone.

Lindsay sounded overjoyed.

"Why, what a welcome surprise! A pleasure to hear your voice again, where are you? It's ages since I've heard from you, how are the kids …..?"

The words came tumbling out and flowed all the more rapidly once Melani said.

"The family's fine, thanks and guess what – we're actually right here in Oakville!"

With a hint of curiosity, she asked in a cheerful voice.

"Does that mean I'll be able to see all of you? I've been looking forward to meeting your husband and the kids for such a long time!"

"Both kodi and Pete, especially Pete had heard so much about the red-haired beauties, he can hardly wait to see them," said Melani.

"Actually, we're quite near your office and knowing how hot the market is at this moment why don't we meet there? That is if you have no other engagements."

Lindsay thought for a moment. "Do give me an hour and I'll try to change my appointment or try to get someone to stand in for me. We help each other when someone needs a favour. You bet I am not going to lose this opportunity!"

In fact, they had been lucky to catch Lindsay at home at all, so they agreed to give her an hour. Soon Kodi and Pete came up with the way to fill in the time.

CHAPTER 6

THE SHOPPING SPREE

Seeing his parents in a good mood and remembering that it was his birthday, he decided to take advantage of the situation.

"Why don't we look around these shops mum?" suggested Kodi as Pete seconded the idea and convinced his father to accompany him.

They walked around doing some window–shopping. "Well we don't want to stay around for women's stuff, do we Dad?" asked Pete.

As Melani and Kodi came around the corner they saw a smart outfit which was just about Kodi's size in one of the shop windows.

"Mum shall we go in?" It didn't take Kodi a moment before she was in the trial room. She came out wearing the off-white suit that was in the window. It looked gorgeous on her.

"You surely look lovely, darling!" uttered Melani.

"Then you like it, Mum? Can I buy it?" Pleaded Kodi.

"We'll do that later, if we have the time," teased Melani.

After she had got back into her own clothes, she came out looking pretty sulky and disappointed. Kodi was utterly disappointed.

Melani then told Kodi that she had to go the bank.

"Kodi, I don't want you to get bored. There's an exclusive Art Galery just round the corner I am sure you'd love that. Why not take advantage of this opportunity?"

She knew how much Kodi loved paintings. This brought a smile back to Kodi's face. She then walked into a small Art Gallery where a Goya exhibition was on. Then Melani made her escape to get Kodi's outfit, which she quickly took to the car. She wanted to give Kodi a surprise.

Later, when they were all in the car, it ruffled Kodi to see her brother examining a packet. It seemed as if only he was in the limelight and getting all he wanted, which put her out completely.

"So you've bought something and I haven't!"

"Well, it's my birthday, why do you think we've done this trip?"

But he couldn't bear to see that look on her face any longer.

"Oh really, he retorted, what's this then….?" Kodi's face immediately lit up. She tore open the package and gave a little scream of delight... "Oh Mum… Pete.!" she mouthed looking from one to the other.

Pete then showed them what he had bought.

"This is my birthday present! I rarely get the opportunity of choosing my own, so I decided that now I am old enough to do just that."

Pete was just sixteen! He was growing up and promised to be a dashing young man. He was not very tall with brown wavy hair and the most beautiful brown eyes. He always attracted the looks of a number of girls. You could see them as they nudged each other when they passed by him.

"Gio, I think we 'd better hurry now or we'll be late for our appointment."

With that they made themselves comfortable in the car and drove to Lyn's place.

CHAPTER 7

INTRODUCTIONS

*L*indsay was not very tall and rather plump but she had such lively blue eyes!

Friendly and helpful, she never said,"No", if she could give someone a hand.

She was already in her car waiting for them. Melani then introduced the whole family. They took to her instantly. This is Pete, he's in high school.

"Aren't you a good-looking boy! And this is Kodi, in her tenth year. You're a really handsome family! My daughters would never forgive me for not inviting you in. They aren't home yet but will be shortly. So would you guys like to come in, we could have coffee and meet the kids later."

Gio immediately refused. "We could do that another time. Didn't you say you were short of time too? But we would like to have a look at some houses around here, why don't we do that?"

"Well of course, that would be my pleasure and should you find something you like here, it would definitely give us all the more reason to meet again. So, I not only get to meet my dear friend and her family but I also get to do business with her. Wouldn't it be wonderful if you decided to move here? Then we could all meet as often as we wished." she answered excitedly.

CHAPTER 8

OAKVILLE

"I'd better take you to the office and see what there is on the market. I know that we recently got a couple of beautiful houses. I didn't get to see them myself but I heard the agents raving about one of them."

"Gio, would you like to see some open houses?" asked Melani.

"Don't start that now! We have only come here to spend the day, do you remember?" He answered.

"Gio, you've forgotten that my great friend Linsay Bloomfield whom you just met, lives here and I would so love to visit her, more often. I hardly get to see her. Often I have to refuse her invitations to parties. For that matter we hardly go anywhere. Besides, you would enjoy meeting her husband, who is quite a sport. He has been looking forward to meeting you. At this moment he is away, in Japan on a business trip."

Both the kids chimed in, "Why would you like to disappoint mum, she hardly goes anywhere, so Dad please, why can't we? It's such a beautiful place! We aren't going to buy any houses here, or are we?" He teased. They both seemed to be captivated with everything they saw. Generally the water front was the greatest attraction, for everyone coming here.

Oakville was supposed to be one of the most beautiful, exclusive, residential areas in Ontario. And some of the best Golf- courses where World - Championships have been held. So they decided to visit Linsay. I think I'll give her a call and see if she's at home. Melani then went to the nearest telephone booth.

The moment she got Lyn on the phone she exclaimed,

"What a welcome surprise! How wonderful to hear your voice, lady, where are you? It's ages since I've heard from you. I hope that you and your family are well!"

Her voice burst with excitement when she recognised her friend's voice.

"They are well and guess what? We are actually here in Oakville!"

"Now that can't be true, why didn't you call me earlier and let me know you were coming to town. I could have made arrangements to find someone to replace me at work and we could have planned something together. Well, it's so like you, but I am not going to complain."

These words flowed from her, all in one breath.

Then she added with curiosity, "Will I get to meet your dear family, at last? I hope they aren't going to waltz away, while we are together as I have been looking forward to meeting them for a very long time. Do you remember all the great promises?"

"Well, I am with the family. Both Kodi and Pete, especially Pete had heard so much about the red-haired beauties, that they can hardly wait to see them." Said Melani.

"We are actually quite near your office, so why can't we meet there, if that's alright with you? We know that the Real Estate market is hot now, and since you must be extremely busy, that could be the best bet. Would that suit you? If you have another appointment we could do this some other time. I didn't call you before we left home because we hadn't planned on coming this way. We were actually on our way to Burlington and I was going to call you from there. But now that we are here, let's make the most of it."

"Do give me an hour and I'll try to see if I could change my appointment or get someone else to do it for me. We sometimes help each other, when someone needs favours. And you bet, I am not going to lose this opportunity!"

Fortunately they were lucky to catch Lyn at home. She was a very successful agent. They continued on the phone for a few more minutes and hung up.

CHAPTER 9

THE SHOPPING SPREE

"Why don't we look around these shops mum?" No sooner did Pete say that, soon Kodi chimed in too. So they walked around doing some window shopping. As they came around a corner they saw a beautiful outfit in one of the shop windows which was just about Kodi's size.

"Mum shall we go in there?" It didn't take Kodi a moment before she was in the trial room. She came out wearing an off-white suit that looked gorgeous on her.

"You surely look lovely!" uttered Melani.

"Then you like it, Mum? Can I buy it?" pleaded Kodi.

"We'll do that later, if we have the time," teased Melani. Kodi was utterly disappointed.

After she had got back into her own clothes she came out looking pretty sulky and disappointed.

In the meantime both Pete and his father had walked away saying that they didn't want to get bored, with women stuff. So after fixing a time to meet where the car had been parked they walked away. Half an hour later Melani told Kodi that she had to go to the nearby bank.

"Kodi, I don't want you to get bored, there is an exclusive Art Gallery, just around the corner, I am sure you would love that. Why don't you take advantage, of this opportunity?"

She knew how much Kodi loved paintings. This brought a smile back into her face. She happily left her mother and walked into a small Art Gallery, where they normally held exhibitions.

Melani used this valid excuse to get rid of Kodi. Then she made her escape to get Kodi's outfit, which she soon took to the car as she wanted to give Kodi a surprise.

Later when they were all in the car Kodi was ruffled to see a packet being examined by Pete.

"So you've bought something, and I haven't!" Complained Kodi.

"Well, it's my birthday, or have you forgotten, why do you think we have done this trip?"

"And, oh really!" he retorted, "what's this then?" Kodi's face immediately lit up.

Pete then showed them what he had bought. "This is my birthday present! Since I rarely get an opportunity of choosing my own present, I decided that I am old enough to do that now!"

Pete had just turned 16. He was growing up to become a dashing young man. He was not very tall he had brown wavy hair and the most beautiful brown eyes. He always attracted the looks of a number of girls. You could see them nudge each other as they passed by. Some would openly draw his attention, by saying something, which ruffled him, at times. At other times he'd give them a smirk, in return.

"Giovani, I think we had better hurry now or we'll be late for our appointment." With that they made themselves comfortable in the car and drove to Lyn's place.

CHAPTER 10

INTRODUCTIONS

*L*insay is blonde, she has long wavy hair, and is of medium height. She had sparkling, blue eyes. Friendly and helpful she never knew the word "No", if she could give someone a hand. The family took to her instantly She was already outside in her car, waiting for them.

Melani then introduced the whole family to Lyn. "This is Pete! He's doing his 11th year."

"Aren't you a very handsome boy? And this is Kodi, I presume, doing her tenth. You're quite a handsome family!"

"You must know that they both study in Burnhamthorpe High school!" said Melani.

"My daughters will not forgive me for not meeting all of you as I spoke about all of you a couple of times. They aren't home yet but will be in a short time. For now would you guys like to come in, see my house. We could have coffee, and you could meet the kids later."

Giovani immediately refused.

"We could do that another time. And I don't know if you remember you have very limited time, too.

"Actually Linsay, we would like to have a look at some houses around here. So if it is possible we could do that!"

"Well of course! That would be my pleasure and should you like something here, it would definitely give us all the more reason to meet again. So I not only get to meet my dear friend and her family, but also get to do business with her. Wouldn't it be wonderful, if you decided to move here. Then we could meet as often as we wish and our families would get together as often as we wish." She answered excitedly.

"In that case I'd better take you to the office and see what there is, in the market. I know that we recently got a couple of beautiful houses. I didn't get to see it myself but I heard a couple of agents raving about it.

"Now Melani, why didn't you call me earlier so we could have planned something very special. This is the first time I'm getting to see all of you together. Besides your kids could get to meet my daughters. It's a pity that Garry is out of town again. He travels a great deal.. you know. He is in Japan, at the moment. Quite often we talk about you and he always asks me when he would get the opportunity of meeting the rest of the family. But I can see that Giovani, is in a hurry. We Could do it he next time you come into town.

CHAPTER 11

PENETANGUISHINE

"Kodi and I got to visit them in their summer house in Penetanguishine, along the Georgian Bay about 450miles away from Toronto. All the houses there were laid out around a horse-shoe shape, so that every house had a wide view of the sea. In the centre there was a lawn more sandy than grassy.

Most of the houses were made of logs –rustic looking, comfortable and cosy. There were a couple of pine trees around the house to give it some kind of privacy. There were in groups of eight to ten houses, similar in size, colour and design. The urbanization was quite big. But being a weekend home there weren't many people around.

We had only gone there for three days Monday to Wednesday. We spoke and played some indoor games, late into the night.

I don't know if we disturbed Barry who had to commute to work every day but he never complained. We made sure to stay as far away from his bedrooms.

All the houses had three little rooms, a kitchenette, a living room and a bathroom. There was a big patio in the front of the house, where we usually sat in the evenings, to enjoy the cool breeze blowing from the sea. This was when Kodi got to meet the family. We had a short, but sweet and relaxing holiday, which to me was an and is, unforgettable.

We had a great time laughing and joking a great deal. Early in the mornings we used to go for a stroll along the shore. Once we actually went for a short boat ride. Lyn was not comfortable with having to pilot the boat so we didn't get very far.

"We have to repeat this! But next time, we should plan it ahead of time so we know that all of us are going to be together. All the same I won't complain because I know how busy you are too! This is a miracle! I can't believe that you actually convinced your husband to drive us down there. I know he drives 200 kms. a day to work, so I understand why you always have to stay at home in the weekends.

I'm really glad that you managed to come and see me, even if it's only for a moment. Even if it's only going to be business!" She added pretending to be sarcastic, with a chausy grin. Then walking towards her car she observed how both Kodi and Pete had stopped to examine it.

She could see the look on both their faces.

She asked, "Who wants to ride with me?" Although Pete was a little shy, his curiosity got the better of him - to drive in a Corvette was irresistible.

"Are you going to keep the hood down?" Pete inquired.

"Yes, of course!" Pete's eyes shone with excitement.

"Do you drive fast?" Both Kodi and Pete asked excitedly as they drove with her.

As Gio opened the door to allow Melani into the car he wondered whether it was the right thing to look at houses there. He could see from her expression that she would love, living in this city.

He was soon to discover that it was one of the most relaxing cities he had come to know, in Ontario. This was a city far from the rush and tear of living in Toronto.

Lyn, was pleased to be told, as they were nearing the office that she had, had a last minute cancellation of her appointment.

"Oh, aren't we lucky?" she said to Kodi and Pete, as she turned to hang up the phone.

It all just seems to fall into place. As she drove she kept talking to both the kids who seemed to open to her. They found her a pleasant person to be with. It was clear that she had children and must be a wonderful mother, because they felt very comfortable in her company.

CHAPTER 12

UFT

oth Lyn and Melani used to be the thickest of thieves when they were studying Real Estate, in the University of Toronto, where they met for the first time.

Whenever they got an opportunity, they used to study together.

Lyn recalled how both of them used to go down to the basement in Melani's house. It was not only- well furnished with comfortable furniture but they made sure not to forget the food and drink, to snack between their breaks… those delicious patties which Lyn enjoyed – They usually studied for hours on these rare occasions.

Reading, discussing when in doubt and then long silences when they decided it was time to find their nooks so that they could concentrate with a previously agreed upon period of time, during which time they had to study Law, Mathematics, and Banking. Now and again, they'd take a break now and spend some time on questioning each other. This could go on, from four to five hours, they took maximum advantage of the little free time, they both rarely had.

They sometimes switched houses. Both had their respective families to look after, no doubt.

"It's a pity that Melane was living so far away. I hope they decide to settle down here! I like her children so it would be lovely for my kids too!" thought Lyn.

She told the kids how she got to meet their mum.

CHAPTER 13

DOWN-TOWN OFFICE

*L*indsay's office was down-town in a very chic area. It looked as if it had been build recently, as it was ultra-modern, contrary to most of the surrounding buildings.

Later they were told that it was just a couple of years old. The decor was a combination of the old and the new, mostly with a touch of finesse.

It was clear that Linda was much appreciated in the office. No sooner had they arrived she took them to her room. Just a click on the phone brought one of the secretaries. She handed her a note ordering ice-tea specially, for the children as it had a delicate touch of lemon ice cream. And coffee for the three of them.

Both Kodi and Pete had a twinkle in their eye when they were given their unexpected specialty. She recalled Melani telling her about their tastes, sometime before.

Making sure they were comfortable she went to get the necessary information for them.

A few minutes later, a knock and then Lyn came in with the secretary carrying some files.

"Here are files on the best houses that we have in the market, at this moment!"

Both Giovani and Melani went through them and decided on a couple of houses they wanted to see.

"Here's one which says - Needs to be sold urgently -!" pointed out Lyn. "I like it very much, I just saw it yesterday. The owners have to leave for Montreal by the end of the month. They are open to all offers. Let me check and see if it's possible to get a look at it, today. Sometimes it's rather difficult to do so."

She dials May, "the smart looking secretary.

"Do we have the key for Keel Cresent, in the office?"

"Yes, do you need it, if so, I shall take it to your office. Oh by the way you don't have to give the owners any notice, at all, as the house is empty!"

A few minutes later she joined them.

"Yes, we have no problem and I was also checking on a couple of houses that are in the same area so you can compare houses.

On the way to the house they wanted to visit, Lyn stopped to show them two of the houses she had mentioned.

Although they were quite pretty, nobody in the family were really attracted by either of them. So Lyn didn't hesitate to take them to the house they had originally planned to see.

CHAPTER 14

THE CHOICE

huge, elegant pine tree, set, in the middle of a rock-garden surrounded by a great variety of little bushes of brightly coloured flowers which adorned the entrance to the house… a pleasant welcome sight.

Linsay took out the keys and opened the door with great difficulty. It was a strong Mahogany door with an ornamental brass knocker. They all removed their shoes as was the custom in most of the houses The oak, wooden flooring shone as if recently polished. The perfume of fresh lavender reached their nostrils.

"Isn't this an inviting, refreshing perfume?" commented Kodi as they went through the door.

"You know I was told that they had just renovated the house, not knowing, that they were soon to get a transfer!" said Lyn

Both the kids in unison, "Could we go around the house on our own?"

Melani gave them a look of disapproval which didn't escape Lyn.

Before either Gio or Melani could utter a reprimand Lyn said, "Come on, go ahead!"

Then turning to Melani and Gio she said.

"I don't want the children to get bored. Why should they hang around us. Besides they would also have something to comment on, their likes and deslikes."

Much to the irritation of their parents.

"They seem to be very responsible and intelligent, I can see how well you've brought them up!" added Lyn reassuringly when she saw the expression on their faces.

"They surely entertained me on the way here. Often we parents underestimate our children's capacity. They seem to be pretty mature in their arguments and at times they come out with such eye-openers that makes you realise that we should take more time to listen to our children. Don't forget I've got three children myself. They wouldn't like to tag behind us! We must bore them with our mundane talk. You must also know that they could give their own feedback on everything they see, later. This could help you make better choices.

"Children today are very capable and know exactly what they want and know to differentiate between what's good and bad. We have to give them a chance of voicing their opinions, too! I hope I don't seem to be giving you a Sermon. It's just that we parents sometimes find it hard to give them responsibilities because we are too afraid that they would do something we dislike. Don't worry they are not going to destroy the place."

Now to the spacious living room –6.5mts wide. It was again of polished wood. It had a pale pink, touch.

Huge French windows with the most beautiful tapestry through which filtered the sunlight filling the room with great cheer.

They had to draw the blinds to see the beauty of the tapestry. Just one look around made them realise that this house belonged to a well-to-do family.

The windows and the wood trimmings were of natural oak. To the right of the living room the windows formed a gentle half-circle of about 4.5 mts. long. There were two other windows where there was a dining table with six chairs. The curtains were all made of delicate pale pink lace. No doubt they were all custom-made and of a high quality so as to blend with the whole ambience giving it the touch of luxury and comfort everyone would love to have in a home.

A white gliding door opened to an immaculate, white kitchen. This was on a lower level about half a metre. All the appliances and the delicate curtains were in white.

"Everything you see here is included in the price." Commented Lyn.

She then took them to the huge wooden deck. There were four chairs outside.

Overlooking the kitchen window, was a beautiful enclosed garden, with a pool on the left hand side. It sparkled in the sunshine - blue, crystal - clear and inviting. We could see the bottom of the pristine pool in the sunlight. The rays of sun played tricks with the shadows from the couple of nearby trees that gently swayed in the gentle breeze sending little ripples that went on to form circles as the water gently moved with the light breeze.

Turning around Linsay could see temptation written all over the kids faces.

Melani didn't have to tell them anything. It was clear they hadn't come prepared with no change of clothes.

But both Pete and Kodi kept looking anxiously at the pool. They very much wanted to slip off their shoes and hang their feet in the pool. On a warm day like that it surely looked enticing. After the air-condition, it surely was warm outside. But one warning look from their parents told them that nothing was possible.

"We'll go out later after we have seen the rest of the house." Walking back into the kitchen, Linsay pointed out to the white railing on the left. This overlooked the nook down below. "Doesn't that look real cosy!"

There was a beautiful fireplace which had two divisions for firewood. The whole wall was lined with wood which had some very beautiful paintings. All around the nook there were built-in sofas with great big fluffy cushions. A storm door led to the garden outside.

Once again they walk back through the living room and down the short flight of stairs to the little hallway which seemed to divide the house into three parts.

On to the right –the living room and kitchen, on the left all the bedrooms and bathrooms.

At the end of the hall –the nook was at ground level, which led out to the garden.

Melani thought that was neat.

"If someone was asleep and didn't wish to get disturbed, this was a great solution!"

They took the stairs, two metres away from the hall and walked up a flight of stairs up to the bedrooms.

There were three of them, which were tastefully decorated.

The master bedroom was on the right. It was decorated in pale salmon with blinds that had tiny little flowers of a slightly stronger colour with pale-green leaves. The sheers were off-white. This was a very spacious room. A two-metre bed would easily fit in. The flooring was covered with plush, salmon wall-to wall carpets. On one side there were mirrored cupboards, from ceiling to flooring, with sliding doors.

There was an en-suite bath which had a bath with mirrored sliding doors from the floor to the ceiling, a toilet on one side and a washbasin that was all in salmon, too.

The flooring was made of tiles, impeccable and of a matching colour. There were cupboards for toiletries and towels. There was a window on one side, so the bathroom was equally bright and cheerful. Every window had a different view of the surrounding neighbourhood.

Lyn, read the expression on Melani's face.

"I can see you've fallen in love with this place. It really is lovely. Rarely do you come across something like this, where you could walk in and live without having to spend a cent on renovations. I wouldn't like to push it, but if you are seriously thinking of moving to Oakville I would recommend that you don't delay on making a decision, on this property, at this price.

It has just come on the market, not more than two days ago. Only a couple of agents got to see it and your family - the first people to be shown the property. I don't think they would have put this on the market, at this price, if they hadn't the problem of time. Mrs Timothy was terribly disappointed that they had to leave at such a short notice. Her husband has no time to come back and forth from Calgary, once they leave."

"Yes, of course, I just love this place. We always wanted to move to Oakville. Secondly this would also give us some extra money as property prices in Etobicoke have gone up a great deal. This is much cheaper than we had expected, but we would still have to weigh the pros and cons. Would it be possible to give us a couple of days to sleep over it?" asked Melani.

She knew that Giovani never liked to rush headlong into anything. But at the same time they didn't have to be told that such deals don't often occur.

Looking for a loophole to convince Geo she asked,"Do you think there would be a possibility of getting them to lower the price?"

"I am sure they will, but it would depend on how fast you would close, on the property!"

"If I were you I wouldn't drag this. The best excuse not to show the property to others is by saying that you are looking into the financing and need a couple of days. That's the best I can do for you, and at my own risk.

"So call me, with your decision and your offer and I'll do my very best. If you do choose to move here, you would love this city. It's one of the most peaceful, residential areas in the whole of Ontario, with great communications and a higher level of life. The school is just a hop, skip and jump from this house. I saw it on our way here. The park is also nearby! "Should the kids need to go down-town there's a bus two blocks down the road.!"

"We'll have to talk about it!" said Melani

In the meantime both Kodi and Pete were deciding on which of the rooms were going to be theirs. They could be heard, arguing about it. No sooner had they arrived at the other rooms, they realised why they were arguing.

There was a distinct difference between the two rooms. One of them had been decorated beautifully for a baby, not for a teenager. Pete being older no doubt had already chosen the more beautiful room. It was laid out all in blue with a touch of maleness in it.

"Mom, I'm the only one who doesn't have a room suitable to my taste! The wall-paper and the curtains are all covered with Walt Disney characters and animals," said Kodi looking very disgruntled.

"All the more you should be pleased because you are going to be the only one who's going to have an opportunity of making a choice as to the colour you would like to have for your room. You get to decorate your room to your taste, lucky girl! Besides, You also have this beautiful view which nobody has!" With this Lyn was able to bring back a smile to her face.

They went through the other two rooms feeling very pleased with it all. No doubt the third room would have to be re-decorated with the exception of the flooring.

"Now let's go downstairs," said Lyn as she led the way down the stairs to the little hall that separated the bedrooms completely from the rest of the house. "You saw the nook from up stairs. Now we could go through there, to the garden Then she opened the sliding doors that led out to a small patio.

No sooner had the shutters been opened, than the sunshine filled the room.

"Now this is glorious!" gasped Melani. There were numerous bushes that was a blaze of colour, tastefully scattered around the pool with enough walking space that was separated by a paved walk of red tiles 1.5 m. wide all around the pool. There was a couple of fruit trees one on side of the house which was near a patch that had been prepared for a little kitchen garden. Onions and garlic sprouts could be seen pushing their way out of the earth. There was another patch divided off and covered with a mesh.

"Would you like to taste these most delicious straw-berries?" interrupted Lyn. She removed the mesh to pluck a couple of them, offering them to Kodi and Pete, who were conveniently standing beside her as both of them were on the point of doing so.

Lyn being a mother missed nothing, especially, when she realised how they both hesitated. Pete very generously offered his to his mum, before he tasted it.

She raised her eyebrows and took it with a smile. "That's so unlike Pete," she thought, he must be growing up because most often he is very selfish.

"I quite agree with you, they're really very sweet!"

They then walked all round the garden through a gate that led to the front garden. There were two huge spruces in the front of the house.

"I don't know if you had remembered that!" said Lyn as she returned through the gate, towards the garden and walked towards the deck.

While they sat talking on the deck (they were four comfortable deck chairs beside a table and a barbecue) A squirrel was seen approaching.

As Lyn was opening her bag, she asked.

"Pete and Kodi, would you like to feed the squirrels?" offering them some peanuts.

No sooner had they sat on the floor of the deck, than the squirrel approached Kodi who had already had her hand outstretched.

It gently took the peanut and held it between its paws, and unabashed it took it to its mouth and soon began to nibble, at it. Before long we could see the shell, in tiny pieces all around and the nut was nibbled away, as it approached Pete for another. It went from one to the other, allowed them to pet it, until it discovered that there was no more and then ran up the tree in the twinkling of an eye.

"This surely looks unbelievable! The children look so excited about this place and so do I. Now it would all depend on Gio. I suspect he likes the place too."

"We have heard a great deal about Oakville. An added plus would be that we would also have some extra money because our present house would fetch quite a good price." She then turns to Gio.

"What do you think of the property?"

"Yes, it's pretty good and of course it's cheaper than I had expected. But we would have to think about it."

Turning to Lyn, he asked, "Would it possible for us to have some time to think about it. I wouldn't like to make rash decisions."

"Well, I hope that wouldn't take more than a day or two because opportunities like this don't crop up often and you know how bosses are! My only excuse could be that you are studying the financing, so you would need a few days. But please don't delay! I would really love to have you, living here in Oakville. It would be wonderful for our kids too.

About an hour later Lyn suggested that they go, to the lakeshore.

"This is the best time, to be at the waterfront if you wish to see all the boats return. Besides, you can also see the sunset, over the lake."

As they were approaching they could see the great excitement all along the quayside. The boats were gliding towards the shore. They came one behind the other with their glorious coloured sails... the splash of colour that reflected in the water.

The water again was soon catching a tint of red as the sun began to slowly go down. All around there was so much colour and cheer. A few moments later the surrounding area suddenly turned pink, in the twilight.

There was an enormous difference living in big cities and then coming to a residential area like this.

There was so much excitement as children kept running up and down. Others were just strolling along, while still others were busy rolling their sails, pulling their ropes so as to anchor their boats.

Their colourful sails added to the setting sun, their metal poles snatching a few rays of the sun, sending rays of the sparkling sunshine in all directions.

The water kept lapping against the shore and the concrete walls of the piers while the ducks and geese took advantage of the last few moments of the day, before they came to shore.

There they said their goodbyes, promising to keep in touch.

"We'd better hurry before we catch the heavy traffic on the freeway!"

"Good luck, on your decision!" Lindsay called out, as she drove out of the drive.

CHAPTER 15

EXCITEMENT

En-route, the kids kept talking nineteen to the dozen. They loved the house, but they decided not to ruffle their father, so they continued talking to each other. Melani was able to catch snips of their conversation. Pete was trying to give his sister ideas about decorating her room.

"I'll take you to a decorators where you have a wide choice of paper and shutters to match. It is quite near the mall. I'll go with you on Saturday. I'm sure you will go crazy when you see the great variety they have there and you wouldn't know what to choose."

It didn't take long before their voices slowly died down. By the time they reached home a deep silence had fallen. Everyone was tired, so all they had for supper, was a couple of ham and cheese sandwiches with a glass of milk. A quick shower and they were in a deep slumber.

"Let's sleep over this thought!" Gio said to Melani, when they were in bed.

"We shouldn't rush into things. But it would be a good idea for you to check on the possibilities of the sale of our house."

The next day, everyone was up early had breakfast and were soon off to school.

That day Melani didn't have to drag them out of bed.

CHAPTER 16

THE APPOINTMENT

Melani had an appointment with Mr. Paul Gregory who was the Councillor of their school. She decided to leave later, as teenagers are pretty particular of not being accompanied by their parents and not get into such embarrassing situations.

According to them, "We don't need to be taken to school nor feel as if we are being chaperoned. We are too grown up for that!"

Half an hour later, Melani arrived at school making sure that the students had all gone into their respective classes. She didn't want her children to know of her visit. Teenagers were pretty sticky about such things.

Paul was rather stocky, blonde with bright blue smiling eyes. The boys nick-named him Mr. Smiley but they dared not say that to his face as they had a great respect for him and knew where to draw the line.

Although he was rigid about the students following the rules, he always stood by them if they needed any help at any time. He was gentleness itself, in delicate situations. But the students rarely saw him in that light. They knew who the boss was. Some of them were terrified of him. Their interests were his greatest priority. Nothing was too small for him when they were in need.

Melani was very pleased to meet him as her children kept singing his praises. After having discussed her children with Paul she felt more relaxed and happy. Feeling very pleased, she thought of inviting him and his family to their home.

She enjoyed being with the teachers and directors of the school. So she knew how their children were faring on a regular basis. Paul Gregory was such a pleasant person that she decided to invite him and his wife to their home.

CHAPTER 17

THE INVITATION

Two days later she called Paul.

"Both Giovani and I were wondering if you would like to come for dinner to our house," said Melani.

"Why, of course it would be a great pleasure! But let me check with my wife and see if she has other plans." He was taken by surprise. He normally didn't go to people's houses.

He was taken by surprise and it showed on his face, but he looked very pleased.

"I'd love to do so but I 'd better check with my wife and see if she has anything on, if not rest assured, it would be a great pleasure, thank you!"

That evening he called and said that they would be free for that weekend.

The following Saturday she woke up bright and early all prepared to make a very special meal. The house looked spic and span before she went to the kitchen. The day before she had gone shopping. Both Kodi and Pete decided to give a hand. This took her by surprise. Since there was no time for comments, she wanted to get some very tender lamb - her specialty!

Out came her special olive oil from the pantry, which she used to swab the lamb with. She then sprinkled some salt, chopped up some pods of garlic, which she spread under the lamb. She was about to put it into the oven when she remembered the tenderiser, special, non-alcoholic, white wine that had been given to her by a friend from Lifestyles. She sprinkled some of it all over the lamb and then put it into the oven.

She decided to serve mashed potatoes and stuffed mushrooms, together with it. She made some gravy, to be poured over the potato.

Lifestyles, had been their favourite restaurant. They tastefully served the most delicious meals, one could imagine. Being frequent guests there, most of the waiters knew them. Often enough they were encouraged to have the best dishes of the day and were given that little extra attention and now and again a recipe was dished out to them.

It was situated in a very beautiful plaza oriented towards a breath-taking Japanese garden with many Bonsai trees and a blaze of colourful flowers.

One of the cooks working there, once revealed the secret of their cooking – the very special cooking wine exclusive to their restaurant.

Melani couldn't resist asking, "Would it be possible for us to buy some of it?"

"We usually don't sell it, but we could get you a box of twelve, if you come here next week," Said the owner of the restaurant.

Melani used this sparingly and only on special occasions. This was accompanied with some green salad that was made of lettuce, cucumber and tomatoes from her garden. She also added some beetroot and spring onions. She then added some salt, vinegar and olive oil.

For hors -d'euvres she had some very special cured ham – Jamburgo – from Spain. She used it very sparingly It was supposed to be the best cured ham in the market. They usually picked this up from an Italian shop, where they sold most of the food from the Mediterranean. Some asparagus with some home-made mayonnaise was followed by steamed King Prawns with some sauce and veal cutlets.

Gio brought out the red wine that had been kept for special occasions and put it to cool - Campo Viejo – from the Rioja.

For desert she made a lemon pie.

CHAPTER 18

THE ARRIVAL

At 2 p.m. the door- bell rang. Kodi was a bit nervous, but Pete was at the door in a moment. Paul presented his son Dave to him. Soon Melani and her husband came to meet them. After the introductions they were shown to the drawing room.

"It's a pleasure to meet you Marilyn, I've been looking forward to meeting you. I must say you have quite a handsome family. Your husband has been very kind to us. If it weren't for him, I don't know what I would have done." said Melani.

She gave them a warm welcome. It didn't take long before everyone felt very much at home.

Their son Dave seemed to be, very sedate, and rather reserved but it didn't last long. Half an hour later he was chatting as if he had known Kodi and Pete for a long time. Although he was a couple of years older than them they had no problems holding a healthy conversation.

His parents mentioned how responsible he was. Dave was quite tall and pale like his mother, but robust. He was studying Computer Engineering and had just one more year to go. He was actually offered a job in a company already. So he will be working there part- time until such time, he finishes his career.

"He was someone I'd have liked for a son-in-law." The thought crossed her mind not only because his parents sang his praises, but she could see the type of boy he was. No doubt Kodi was still too, young.

He seemed very fond of his parents and made sure that all was well with them, especially his father who, at that time was having problems with his eyes. He had, an operation done but it wasn't a success, so he had to wait a week before he went through it again.

Melani left the children and Gio to take care of them. They showed them around the garden and found a cool spot where they have their drinks. Gio had a martini, while Paul preferred to have a gin and tonic. The two boys had a shandy and Kodi preferred to have just a coke. They all had some calamari fries and olives to snack on.

Melani and Marilyn had a Bloody Mary, mostly tomato juice and just a dash of vodka.

They also had olives and calamari, to go with it.

The table cloth was white and transparent with a few pink flowers here and there. They had serviettes to match. The crockery was Italian. White with gold trimming, a couple of sprigs of tiny red roses with green leaves. The glasses were Bohemia Crystal.

She joined by Marilyn. "Can I give you a hand?" She asked.

"Yes, please I kept the salad for the last minute because I wanted it to be crisp. While I chop the onions, you can cut up the tomatoes, and the beetroot, I'll get prepare the lettuce!"

She added the olive oil, vinegar and salt and then mixed them together. They also had asparagus with mayonnaise. Once this was laid out on the table they were joined by the others and sat out in the open-air, near a Cyprus, nursing their drinks while they chinwagged.

The dinner had been laid in the dining room overlooking the garden and the pool. The first dish was made up of soup - Cheese with cucumber made into a cream which was light and delicious.

This was followed by fresh water boneless trout, which had a filling of shrimps. with some pink cream, poured over it. This was surrounded by roasted, crushed almonds, and a sprig of parsley in the centre. Finally they had roasted lamb with small golden brown potatoes, and some peas. Over it she poured some sautered onions with gravy.

Desert was made of fresh strawberries with cream and some roasted walnuts.

For drinks they had some wine 1990 Rioja (special from Spain) which was kept away for special occasions. The boys had beer and Kodi again preferred to have her coke.

The Dinner was a great success because everyone seemed to have enjoyed their meal.

They were all very cheerful people and made sure to contribute toward a hilarious evening. They left around 12 p.m. extracting a promise that the Giovani family would visit them sometime soon.

"We'll call you a week before, thanks for this delicious dinner and the great company, of course!"

Melani was very tired, as she had spent the whole day on her toes so she went for a shower and was in bed a few minutes later. The next day when she woke up she was surprised to discover that there was not a dirty dish on the table and everything looked spic and span. Gio had woken up early as usual, put the dishes, crockery and cutlery into the dishwasher.

Surprisingly Gio even complemented her on the dinner. It was not like him.

CHAPTER 19

THE ENCOUNTER

Melani was a gregarious person, cheerful and very energetic. Underneath that very cheerful facade, she was very serious, sensitive and creative. She had a restless nature and had to be always doing something or other.

"I don't know the meaning of boredom", she said.

She enjoyed being with people, practising sports, though she wasn't really good at it. She loved playing tennis and going swimming.

She met Giovanni, at one of the parties, held by Eatons, a department store in Toronto, Canada. It was organised every year, in summer time, for all it's staff and guests on invitation They no doubt had to buy a ticket, tho' this wasn't opened to the general public. This was to be a great Dinner- dance. Besides there were prizes too. They normally had a very good band and so the music was excellent. The party was quite informal but for the couple of speeches and prize distribution – These were given to the outstanding workers, or to those who were retiring that year.

No doubt an analysis of the results of the company was publicly made. The staff who, had done outstanding work received prizes and the Company President thanked everyone for working towards the success of the company.

Giovanni was born in Genova, a coastal town in Italy and had been working in a construction company, with Oswaldo and Valdo – two brothers. They had a sister named Gina, who had been working for Eatons and that was how they got to come to that party. She insisted on them going to it. One of them had an eye on Gio. They had seen him with their brother and sometimes tried to convince him to bring Gio to the house.

Elegant, as most Italians were, both the brothers looked outstanding. Giovanni was wearing a bluish, grey pin-stripped suit. He had light brown eyes, which seemed to give out, a few sparks of gold, every time he smiled. Being a cheerful person he often broke into laughter.

He seemed to be a little distracted – lost in thought! But, for a fleeting moment when he cast a glance at Melani, it seemed to hold. Her voice quivered as she softly whispered to her sister, who was surprised to find her sister so flustered.

But soon she was to discover why. Everyone were served drinks and snacks at their tables. This was one of those moments when people got to meet old friends they hadn't seen for a long time. So there was a great deal of chatter everywhere.

Later dinner was announced and they fell into a queue. There was a quite a spread of food, prepared to suit all tastes, as there were people of all nationalities. Canada has a Multicultural society, so they made sure that everyone was happy. Once dinner was over, everyone moved over to the ballroom where the welcome sound of the band was heard.

The Master of Ceremonies then took over. He said that he wanted to see all the couples on the floor, in his words, "Once again welcome to our annual show. It's nice to see all the old and new faces. Make sure you have a wonderful time. I guess you all deserve it, and that's why you're here. We've got some wonderful music for you so we wish to see everyone on the floor. We also have some games but that will come later. Now let's give the band a hand."

Everyone joined in applauding them. It didn't take long before the band began to play. Soon some couples went to the floor.

Melani was sitting near her friends Janet and Malcolm who she hadn't seen for quite some time. Janet had a sprained ankle and could hardly move.

"I just can't resist coming to these parties as this is the only way I get to see all my friends. Malcolm was dressed elegantly, he looked a bit stiff and starched and seemed to be very serious. An autocrat who always felt he had to control the whole situation. Janet was quite the contrary. A very delicate looking person, very refined and sweet. Everyone wondered how she could handle her husband, so they weren't surprised when they got separated. It took Janet 15 years of intolerance, to decide to leave him. Frankly speaking everyone were happy for her.

But they soon helped us pick up news of the past few months. Gossip was part of these parties. He sometimes came out with anecdotes of various situations that happened, at work or during work. Being a cop He was acquainted with the ways of the world and had, many funny experiences to keep the group laughing. No doubt excluding the gruesome stuff that he had to face on a daily basis. This no doubt marked his personal life. Janet didn't seem to be happy with him. "The same ole' story she used to say nothing ever changes!"

"Why don't you both get some councilling?" asked her friends. That of course was something beyond reach. He was the Macho – man – the perfect person. There was no way someone was going to tell him how to run his life.

They were immersed in a joke Malcolm was saying when "Excuse me, I hope I haven't disturbed you, would you like to dance?" he asked looking, my way, said Melani. She looked a bit flustered but pleased at the same time but couldn't resist a smile when she heard his accent. "It had a special music to it. I found it irresistible," she commented later, to her sisters who were quite keen on hearing about all that had happened at the party. A couple of them giggled.

"You are pretty drawn towards that guy, that we hardly got a word with you, as we didn't want to get in your way!" Melani recalled those moments. He looked at me with a twinkle in his eye.

"Did I pronounce your name correctly?" he asked, as he tried to repeat her name, after she had told him.

She blushed when she realised that he was watching her very closely, observing her every reaction.

"I think he's rather playful, more mischievous – a big tease no doubt, because he constantly wore a smirk, and that twinkle in his eyes every time he said something, that set a spark that set me on fire!".

Immediately one of her sisters interrupted her, "I'd be very careful if I were you, he's too glamorous, to be trustworthy! He looks too handsome to being someone who'd enjoy settling down to a home life. Look at the number of women who seem to, not take their eyes of him, so sister darling you'd better look elsewhere!"

When Melani heard this, she decided that his behaviour just didn't worry her. She wasn't desperate but she was going to enjoy herself as much as she could.

"Of course there was no doubt about that. I'm sure he realises that he is tremendously popular, but doesn't seem to care! All I know is, that he's a likable person. I've just met him and I'm not going to be a fool to wear my heart on my sleeve, you should have known me better! There's nothing bad about liking a person, is there? Besides I think that you're mistaken about him.

"He's quite a serious person," she unconsciously defended him.

All this conversation took place in the powder room.

Much to the chagrin of the others, he spent all evening sitting beside Melani. If they weren't talking they were dancing They seemed inseparable. He didn't give anyone else an opportunity to even get close to her, which one of her brothers found irritating. Neither did he ever cast a glance at all the other ladies who tried their very best to catch his attention, in vain. Melani happily felt sure, in her heart, that he was equally carried away. She found him extremely entertaining. There was something about him that told her, he wasn't playing games with her and that he was fed up of most of the highty flighty girls that most often tried to draw his attention.

"I am sure what added to the spice was that she also had a spattering idea of his language, which must have surprised him," added one of her sisters. She didn't want her sister to get carried away. So, together they laughed at each other's pronunciation. Recalled

Melani. But unaware of what the others had thought, he felt right from the instant he set eyes on her that he was determined to get married to her. So their courtship hardly lasted more than six months before they got married.

"Melani, I don't want you to run away and hide, after this party and forget this encounter. I would like you to meet the only family member I have here my brother Tino and of course I would also like you to meet, my friends. We are having a small party, next Saturday. Do you think you could come. I know it's too sudden, but I shall call you on Wednesday. That should give you enough time to decide! I shall be looking forward to a positive answer, so please don't let me down."

CHAPTER 20

GIOVANI

On Wednesday at about 8 p.m. he called.

"Hello, Giovani here, may I speak to Melani, please." He sounded rather nervous.

"I hope she doesn't turn me down," He kept telling himself.

"Melani a call for you – you have Romeo on the line," her sister teased.

When she came on the line, she was equally nervous and excited, at the same time.

"Yes, Melani speaking!" she said.

"Would you be coming to our small party? All my friends are looking forward to meeting you and so is my brother and sister. I told them that I didn't quite like the idea of sharing you with them, but I guess I have no other alternative, but to do so! I hope you won't let us down."

"Yes, I will, but I hope you don't mind if my sister goes along with me!" She sounded a bit doubtful. At the same time she just didn't want to go alone.

"Oh, that's no problem, do bring her along. The More, the merrier! I shall be there to pick you up at about 7:30 p.m.

"Well, he surely sound serious about you. One of my Italian friends, at work told me that this is a sign of wedding bells. They never invite you to their homes unless they have a great interest in you. As for Gio, he has no family except his brother, so there goes it and friends. Ah! Ah! I guess he's looking for approval from the rest of his crowd. Don't you think so? He surely surprises, me!"

This is how she got introduced to the Italian world.

At first it was rather uncomfortable as she was being scrutinised by everyone. The Italians were supposed to be clickish and they generally didn't marry outside their community. The families were very united and stuck together thru' thick and thin. Melani and her sister were the only girls from out of the community and soon discovered that there was someone vying for her position.

This girl, called Maria was very beautiful. She had very sharp features, dark- haired, shoulder –length and bewitching, dark eyed. She did her very best to patronise Gio in vain. Whenever she could she would cut Melani of. At first this made her feel very disconcerted and found it hard to ignore her and pretend that she didn't notice their rivalry.

But Gio seemed to have eyes for no one, except herself. So she decided to ignore Maria.

This gave her security and she began to relax and enjoy herself. It didn't take long before friends realised why Gio was crazy about Melani. They soon took to her.

"Melani could make a suitable partner, for Gio", Tino. One of his friends commented to another, which Melani overheard. Her friendliness became so catchy that the tension soon disappeared.

There was a lot of laughing and joking. At times she found it hard to understand, their jokes but this didn't keep her from participating. Now and again they were in splits. Sometimes she had to guess what they were saying.

On the whole the sisters had a wonderful there. Gio went out of his way to make sure that Yvonne was also having a great time.

She soon learnt how very important family life meant to the Italians.

"Most of the families, lived with their grand-parents, parents and children in enormous houses. Seeing her frightened expression and he overheard what they had been telling her, he added quickly.

"Don't worry, this won't happen to us. We would have our own house all to ourselves."

This took her by surprise as he took it for granted that, they would get married. Strange as it may seem neither did she feel any different. They got on well. It seemed as if they were made for each other.

"It must be difficult for someone new, to enter such a family and live together!" asked Melani.

Yes, she was madly in love with him and overly excited with the present situation, but this was going too fast for her to grapple the whole scenarial.

"If I'd have problems, I guess I would have to answer to everybody, is it?" Melani stammered.

"Get rid of that frown and let me kiss them, away.

As he said it, his lips slightly brushed her forehead. She turned completely red as suddenly everyone turned in their direction. He had lost his head and seemed to have forgotten that there were more people around.

"Are you sure, you wouldn't want to go back to Italy and live with your family?"

"No, my love I have been living here for the past 15 years – this is home for me!" He said.

CHAPTER 21

HUMBLE BEGINNINGS

Gio had been dating Melani for a couple of months, now. It was one of those cold Saturday evenings, they had just had the first snowfall - the 27 October and the sudden cold Alaskan winds began to blow.

"Shall we go out to dinner. I would like to take you to this queer-looking restaurant, which is very cosy and beautiful "Pietro's Dining", they serve excellent Italian food. The owner is a friend of mine and I am sure he will be pleased to see you. He always called me "The confirmed bachelor!"

"I would like to show him that he's mistaken and that I was waiting for the right person to come my way. Yes, my patience has been rewarded, don't you think so?" He asked for her affirmation, on the phone as he continued to chat.

"Don't you think it's high time I got rid of those mistaken ideas about myself. I have to show him that it was well worth waiting! Having to have waited all this period of time, to have met someone like you, is something I will not change for anything in the world. I can hardly wait for the evening." See you soon.

That evening, around 7 p.m. he came home to pick me up. He had his arm around me as the drastic change from the house on to the street sent a shiver through me. "Now isn't that better!" he said as he opened the car door and let me into it. He had the heater going so it was quite comfortable.

While they waited for the meal to come, he said, "I must tell you about my humble beginnings. I came here with Guiseppe. We were both teenagers, when one of the neighbours told us about Andre.

"Do you know Andre? He has just come back, from the new world and says that life there, in North America is just wonderful – a great place to live! If you want to work, there is work and they pay you very well. But most of all, they pay you!"

So my friend Pietro and I wanted more information as we were very keen on improving our lives. We weren't satisfied with what we were doing. In simple words we were ready for a change. All prepared to go through all kinds of adventure, if necessary. We were both daring and far from lazy. This was the year 1962. We had just completed 15. There was only a few days difference between us.

A few days later we happen to see him, walk past us in the street. Yes, he drew a lot of attention. A new face, fashionably dressed. In other words, he looked successful. Both of them simultaneously said, "Why can't we do something?" Gio said with a determination which said there was no other way out.

"We are young and strong. Yes, we don't have the money, but we could work in, as many jobs and try and save every penny. No more beers" Pietro echoed being in the same mood. "He is a home-town boy. I am sure he wasn't any different from us, at our age. So why can't we?"

That was when the two of us decided to go to America. We searched for as much information as we could get. We knew that it wasn't going to be easy, but once we decided on going, our priority was to go, come what may. We had been brought up in poor families, but we had a dream and we kept that dream alive by meeting and talking about it, in detail, every day. We swore that we were going to this country – the promised land – the land of milk and honey.

Everyday we'd get together, after work and try to work out a plan – easy, it wasn't - the major problem boiled down to money for our ticket. So we took all the odd jobs that came our way, making sure to spend as little as possible on our daily needs. The two of us very much kept to ourselves. This was the only way to avoid wasting even a cent. At first our friends laughed at us but later realised that we were serious about what we wanted to do and gave up on us, as two people with an impossible dream. That life on the street wasn't for us.

I mentioned this to my grandmother. Until then she didn't tell me that she knew Andre's mother very well. Now that she mentioned that, a small hope began to grow within me. True to her word the following week, she donned her best gown and went to visit them. At first she felt, she couldn't go inside, but now that she had walked all the way uphill, it didn't seem intelligent to walk back without fulfilling what she had come here for.

So, she rang the door-bell. She was determined not to send her grandchild without making sure he had a place to go to and a job, if possible.

Of course she received a warm welcome. "How are you Angelina," she asked as she opened the door.

"It has been a long time since I have seen you, what brings you up, here. I hope all is well with you and your family?" She plied her with questions. "Please sit down, you must be tired. Let's have something together."

After having served her capuccini and some snacks Angelina decided it was time to bring out the subject of her grandson.

"Sabrina, I don't know if you know my grandson Giovani. He is going on sixteen and is a very hard worker.

The other day he came to me and asked me to find out, if there would be any possibility of your son helping him and his friend Pietro, to go to America. I know it doesn't depend on you, but I thought that if you casually mention that to Andre, maybe he would be of some help. Even if he can't help personally, at least he could tell them how to go about it."

"Well, I'll try and talk to him. Since his arrival here, he has had many similar requests. He has done very well for himself, but as you know nothing comes easily to anyone. He really had to work his way up, with great difficulty. All the same, it would be better if you ask your grandson to come here with his friend. I will send you a note after I have spoken to him. Yes, I have seen Giovani and his friend. They look like two people who are not lazy and very formal kids. Yes, I promise you, I will do my best. I know that since your husband's accident things haven't been going well for you. But don't worry, you just have to give him some time. It would be nice if the two boys came up here around 6 p.m. on Saturday. He's usually here at this time.

Both the boys were filled with exuberance. "This is the first step towards our dream", commented Gio They were so excited that they arrived there earlier than they were supposed to. Andre saw them coming up the hill and opened the door. He personally didn't know them.

"Well boys, come on in. What would you like to drink?" he invited.

"Well some water would be just fine," said Pietro. Gio nodded too. They swallowed the water very fast as they were very thirsty. Besides being a warm day, they had come a long way, up hill.

"My mother had been speaking about you. Now are you sure you really wish to go through this? Do you have any money for your ticket? Have you saved up anything, for expenses?" He soon realised that they did not have much. Gio picked up courage and said "We have a couple of jobs and we have saved every penny. In a couple of months we should have the money, at least for the ticket. If not, we are both strong, we could work our way on the boat, too.

Andre picked up from there, "Do you think it's going to be easy to find jobs there. Is it very expensive to find a place to live or is it possible to find a place?"

"Well my mother and I have been discussing this over and over again. She mentioned that both your mother and mine had been good friends for long time, but after they got married their lives changed. Each time they became busier and busier and slowly but steadily the ties were lost.

I've decided that I am going to help you with just the basics. You will have to find the money for the ticket one way or other. Maybe you could speak to the boat –people and work your way. Because if you have to wait to earn your money for the ticket, there won't be time. I shall be leaving here in six weeks.

Once that is done I'll give you a place to stay, for a short period of three months and also a temporary job offer so that you can enter the country legally. Once you are there, it all depends on you, to look for a job. I'll give you some references. But be very careful of what you do. But most of all you will have to work very, very hard. Now do you have any questions?"

"Is it true that it is easy to find a job there?" asked Gio.

"Yes, if you are prepared to work". Andre said

They thanked him and returned to their homes much happier. On their way home, they kept hopping and skipping all the way. Each one went their own way, pensative. "Neither of us could sleep that night."

On arriving home, my mother was waiting to hear all that had happened in Andre's house.

"Is she going to help you?" She was pleased with all that he said and knew that she was going to lose her son temporarily. But if it meant for his improvement, Why not?"

She had always suspected that her son would leave sometime or other as he was a born fighter. His friend wasn't any different. So she encouraged him, by putting in her grain of sand. She told him that they had some savings, not very much but it would help towards the trip. An old lady, who was very fond of my parents took me under her protection and later my friend. She send us on many errands and also gave us some odd jobs around the farm. This also helped me earn some money, for the trip."

"Much against my wishes I decided that I had no alternative but to accept my mother's savings. I promised myself that I would work very hard and return that money and also help them for a period of time to raise their level of life."

"I didn't want my parents to suffer as much as they did, so I was determined to go ahead with our plans. My mother always knew about my intentions, she was worried, but at the same time wanted the very best for me. She encouraged me greatly with a smile tho' I knew she that she must have been crying, at night sometimes. All the more it made me realise that I had to carry out my plans with a brave heart. This would be the only way to help myself and also help change my parent's life for the better, which I knew was possible.

"I am the second child in the family. My father was a fisherman. He went out to sea everyday. I remember one day there was a terrible storm and his boat couldn't be found and we were terrified that he was dead with the others. But fortunately they were saved by other fisherman except for one of them who got drowned.

"It's a miracle that we are alive!" They said when they were found, in the early hours the next day. Those days were tough, but we children learnt at an early age to fend for ourselves, doing all sorts of jobs. Life at that time was difficult for nearly everyone.

"Much to my disappointment, my friend Pietro couldn't go with me as he fell ill just a fortnight before we left. But a year later, I sent him a ticket and he was able to join me. Yes, Andre was true to his word. He gave me a place to stay. It was tiny, but for me, it was a great luxury. It didn't take long before I got a job and looked for a place of my own. If it hadn't been for Andre's references, I would not have got a job very easily. Pietro and I meet pretty often. We are both happy to have come here. Every month, I made sure to send my parents something. I used to visit home often, until some years ago. He stopped there.

I saw, a shadow fall over his face. He suddenly looked very sad. There was something, dark and sad, lurking in his eyes. It was an unconscious reaction and I don't think he realised it. But I didn't want to pry and continued listening to him as if nothing had happened.

She suspected that something in his past, worried him greatly. It has left an indelible mark on him and it couldn't have been a pleasant experience.

She tried to put it out of her mind by saying, "I am sure he will tell me about it, in good time."

Just at that moment we were approached by a kindly looking gentleman. He approached Gio with open arms.

A WELCOME SENTENCE IN ITALIAN ......NOW WHO IS THIS GIRL ... ALL IN ITALIAN.

"Melani, meet my dear friend Angelo!" "Angelo, my dear friend, this is my fiancée! With that he put his hands in his pocket and withdrew a box. and then dramatically he went on his knees, "Melani, will you be my wife?"

She was too shocked for words. She turned completely red. He held her left hand, and put the ring on her finger. She was nonplussed and could only nod her head in agreement. His friend hugged them both.

"Thank you for this great privilege! I am now a happy man. I have seen you Gio, through the ups and downs of life and I knew you deserved the very best and I can see you have chosen the most beautiful girl, I have known you to be with. Her eyes tell me that she will take good care of you.

"Melani, this is supposed to be a special moment for the two of us, but I wanted it to be shared and blessed by my best friend. Here, he is brother, father and friend ….. all in one for me.

Just before I left for North America, some people tried to discourage me from going.

"Don't think that you are going to have a great life. You live much better here, although you hardly have much. On the boat only the strongest will survive all the calamities. Maybe only 10 %. People die of typhoid, lack of water and food. Besides the strong attack the weak. People are abused and robbed. So try to be clean. Now this isn't going to be easy when you are on the ship. Most of the people and you will part of them, dirty, cold and ill due to being in the sea for such a long period, without proper food and water."

This terrified us greatly. For a couple of days, we kept to ourselves, worrying a great deal. But soon we got over it. We got together again with renewed energy, this time with an unshakeable decision.

"I am going Angelo, I am going, nothing is going to stop me, are you coming? Yes, we will have all the problems we can and can't imagine, but that is part of life."

The next day Gio went to visit Andre. He wanted to verify the stories he had been listening to. Andre got him something to drink and then told him, that most of it was true.

"But all this had happened many years ago. I personally had it real rough, when I first went there, but don't worry you won't have to go through all that! You can't compare the experiences those people had.

They were the pioneers! They sacrificed to give us a better life. And you bet, you are going to be very happy when you are there.

Beginnings are not easy for anyone. You will miss everything you leave behind, your parents, the home food and the little things, which in the future won't be important at all. That's natural, but you'll get over it!"

"Well to be frank, when I left home for the first time, I had no money. I recall, not a day passed without a visit paid to the warf, where I used to see people huddled around watching the those boats leave for America. Excitement written on all the faces, young and old, some even with their families, carrying what few possessions they had. They didn't look any different from us. I was one of those young faces The only difference being they had managed to find the money to pay for their passage and I didn't. Fortunately, I was given a job by the Captain of the ship. It was a very tough job! Scrubbing, cooking cleaning, anywhere they needed me I had to go. In compensation I got a free trip, free food and was actually given a job on landing on the Captain's recommendation! After that life only became easier. I am very comfortable now.

"We also made it a point to find the joints where the captain and his crew frequented, so we could pick fragments of their conversations.

"It's a pity so many passengers die during the passage and we lose our workers, very often. We should look around for young blood, people who are hardy enough to face these treacherous trips.

"Don't you think that, that's going to be difficult as most of the people leave here because they don't even have sufficient food to eat," interrupted one of them.

This spurred my friends and I to work harder but also making sure we didn't sacrifice our health. We had to prepare for the worst.

One day, we intercepted the rough-looking captain by asking him, "Are you looking for workers on the Boats?" His immediate answer was, "Can you pay your fare, to America?" Both of them spoke in unison. "We have part of it, the rest could be paid by our working on the boat." "Well, come back tomorrow. I will have to discuss this with my mates." We left very satisfied, as he didn't show us any negative signs. Before he left us, he asked.

"How old are you?" This didn't help us in any way as we were only 15, under-aged.

"Would your parents agree to your leaving. Get them to sign a paper to that effect!"

A week later we waved goodbye to our parents and friends and set sail for America – our dream land. We kept our eyes open, watched our surroundings and observed the very old people who seemed to learnt to fight for survival.

"This story brought tears to my eyes", said Melani. The tears kept rolling.

"Don't spoil that pretty face of yours!" he said as he kissed her tears away.

"Now that must have been stupid of me to have told you these unpleasant stories, while we are having such a wonderful time together. I guess I got carried away and wanted to tell you about some of the experiences and that has helped enrich my life.

"I don't want to go into any more details as you can guess the rest. We survived and here we are healthy, wealthy and wise." He ended and I breathed a deep sigh of relief. The happiest day was when we touched Ellis Island where we were given our imigration papers. We were given valid papers to work just like any American. No doubt without Andre's help at first it would have been difficult to find jobs. But once we began the ball rolling, each day was a new day, with a new life and here I am in one piece. Happy to be an American citizen!

They had a great dinner. By the time she got home she was dead tired. Too many things had happened that day. Gio had completely taken the wind from her sails and she felt completely beaten

They seemed to have fallen madly in love with each other and were inseparable.

"This is just infatuation, don't let yourself get carried way with the glamour of this guy. You better be careful with this guy. It's too soon to get married. Six months …. You better be careful. Latin men are awfully possessive. You are going to have a number of problems. Why can't you give it some more time?"

"What had exactly happened to him, that kept him away from home, for such a long time.? I knew he was about to tell me about it, if that Angelo didn't come in at that moment!"

"Although I am terrified, I am very much in love with him and I know that he is being sincere. Yes, the other day Cathy heard a woman say to her friend, "Be careful of the man you are going to marry, he is a womaniser! You will not be happy with him!"

Melani didn't enjoy hearing those things but at the same time nothing could shake her belief in their love and she decided that she was going to accept his hand, without giving it a further thought.

Late July she invited Gio to her place. He officially asked her parents for her hand and the wedding had been arranged for three months later. An autumn wedding had been planned for.

CHAPTER 22

THE WEDDING

"Your sisters and brothers don't seem very keen on having a big wedding. Did they mention it to you? So according to them, this isn't going to be a very big wedding. I met your brother the other day and he said that they had all discussed the wedding and decided that we could use the money toward something more important.

"No doubt I can't understand why. They also said that all we had to do was just get married. They would see to all the arrangements. To me this is not any different from the Italians. Did they mention anything to you. All I know is that they were sometimes rather vague about it. To be frank, I don't care very much for crowds, I'd rather we spent the extra time to be alone with each other and go on a wonderful honeymoon. Would that be fine with you?" Gio spoke hesitatingly.

"We would have to keep the honey-moon for a week later as I have some very important work to be finished. I have a deadline to meet. I got this order only a week ago. But don't worry I shall make up for it a hundred–fold."

She agreed, "that's no problem with me" Melani answered reassuringly.

Frankly speaking she couldn't understand her family!

"I really think wedding celebrations are a complete waste of time. Besides I have a very big family here. Maybe you should ask your parents to come for the wedding. There's lots of room to put them up here."

"I did ask them but since my mum has had a heart operation, she has been advised by the doctor not to travel. I don't want my mother to be left all by herself, at home! They told me that they will call us on our wedding day and that I should take you there so that they would get to meet me. They are very curious about you. I send them a photograph. They seem very pleased with it.

A week before the wedding Melani asked her family how much money was required for the wedding expenses, however small it was going to be, as Gio wanted to foot that bill.

"Giovani, we'd rather, that's if you don't mind, that we took care of the wedding as it's just going to be something very simple with all our family members."

Connie being the oldest approached him. "But we would like to know how many of your friends are going to be present."

He found them to be a genuine bunch of friendly people, who really made him feel very comfortable with them so he agreed with them. He didn't think this worried Melani in any way, as the family were like the thickest of thieves.

But this wasn't the idea of the family, they thought that this should be a very special occasion – a great celebration. They planned to give the two of them a real surprise so it was a well-hidden secret. Melani had no inkling whatsoever of any of the arrangements. They had planned to get rid of them. The day before the wedding. The boys took charge of Gio. He had full faith in them. They told him that it was bad luck for him to see the bride and took him to Thousand Islands, which was quite a relaxing place. There was a small boat there, so they really enjoyed the ride. "It's a pity Melani is not here. I am sure she would have enjoyed this trip!"

"Don't worry, you can always bring her here, when you wish!"

The sisters took care of Melani. One of them in Missauga invited Melani to spend the day with her.

Melani confessed, "I'm happy to get away, as I am terribly nervous." I don't know if I can go through with this wedding. I am really getting cold feet. She said thanking Yvonne.

They got married at the Holy Cross Church. Father Tim served the mass. He was considered part of the family and felt very much at home with them and made things easy for them. No doubt the week before the wedding was very hectic.

The small reception was to be celebrated in Etobicoke. They surely made a handsome couple. Melani wore an off-white silk dress which had a very simple cut with a couple of tiny little flowers made of gold threads, thrown around. This gave her an ethereal look as the dress easily flowed down elegantly, showing her slim contour. Her dark hair was held together with a tiny crown of white roses that held the veil that flowed down to the long train. Her earrings matched her engagement ring, each had a solitaire diamond, a present from Gio. And so did her literally bare neck with a very thin gold chain and a diamond.

Her two little nieces were the flower girls. They looked very cute in pale pink chiffon dresses holding little baskets and kept holding on to the train. Cheryl kept smiling Creshan looked a bit nervous. She was very shy.

Gio wore a stunning dark-blue suit with a very pale blue shirt and a tie that matched. He wore one of the tiny roses from the bouquet in his button hole.

After Mass, Edwin had arranged with the limousine that after their ride they were to return to the church, where he would be waiting for them, to direct them to the hall.

About half an hour later, when the limousine turned into the Inn, Gio interrupted the driver and told him that he was mistaken with the address as they had expected to have the party in the building. They had been shown the day before. But the driver argued with them saying that he was following instructions from the company.

He was to follow the black car, "Why don't you check with driver?"

So Gio got out and was about to say, "There's some mistake here!" When the driver from the black car got out, removed his heavy dark glasses and said, "This way, please!" It was none other than ……

Their surprise knew no bounds as they entered the drive to find Melani's brother waiting outside.

"Isn't there a mistake Melani, the driver has come to the wrong place?"

"Then why is Ed waiting for us?"

When he approached them, Giovani said, "Ed, isn't there a mistake?"

"No, just come in, I think they have arranged for the photographers here. There is an extraordinary garden here! Come this way, we have to go through this hall."

The moment they entered the hall the band struck, "Here comes the bride!"

It seemed as if from nowhere all the family and friends began pouring in. To his great surprise his brother had brought his parents to the wedding. They were very happy to meet Melani. Tears of happiness filled their eyes. The four of them took some time, later, to be alone with his parents. It looked as if everything was planned to perfection. Showers of confetti began falling from the ceiling and everyone began to clap. The huge hall was beautifully decorated with fresh flowers. The tables were arranged all around the hall, so that everyone could be see the bride and groom.

Gio was so taken aback that he turned red, tears of happiness filled both their eyes as neither of them had suspected anything like this. They both hugged and kissed each other and looked shyily at all the rest of the family.

The toast was given by the oldest sister Connie, wishing them all the best.

Gio took over, "No words can express our gratitude. This is just something impossible to believe. You have gone out of your way to make this supposed –to-be quiet wedding into something so grand, that it has taken my breath away. I am sure Melani must feel the same or, would you by any chance have known about this and hidden it from me?" he asked turning to look at her.

"From her expression, I can see that she is as surprised as I am. A very big thank you. I can hardly speak as you have taken the wind out of my sails! Thank you once again!"

The wedding party was a great success.

The dinner comprised of a great variety of Hors' d eaures, followed by seafood and Lamb. The 6-storey wedding cake was sliced and distributed. Later there was a bowl of fresh tropical fruit, with cream poured over it.

"I want to have these special moments with somebody as special as you are, so we'd better go down south, Just the two of us to California and to Nevada, to try our luck in Las Vegas. At last you will get to see the rockies which you had been looking forward to, from there we could travel around to whatever city you wish. I am free for two weeks and I want them to be the best!

Soon the band struck the chord for the opening dance by the Bride and Groom. They just floated down the hall and the others followed suite. He felt comfortable and both of them looked forward to anxiously settling down.

After the wedding, they arrived at the house only to discover that one of the brothers, in the excitement had gone away with the keys. Fortunately, their neighbours who were great friends of theirs, invited them in. Tired as they were, they both took out their shoes and lay on the sofa, until three hours later, one of the brothers cam with the keys.

CHAPTER 23

OAKVILLE

They decided to buy the house, they had seen in Oakville, very much against the wishes of Melani's family. They were terribly disappointed to lose their sister in a way. "We aren't going to be very far away, don't worry we'll visit you as often as we can.!"

"What will you do when you are bored? Why don't you think about it very carefully? Most of them were upset and in a way Melani hadn't realised at that time the repercussions.

After the first couple of months the novelty began to wear out when she realised that it wasn't as easy to visit her family as often as she would have liked to. She even missed her friends. It was a forty-five minutes drive to visit them, but now there was no turning back.

Driving was one of her passions. She just loved to spread her wings and take off. It gave her a sense of freedom, and heped her relax, especially on the highways. So it was a mode of transport she abused. "All you wish to be, is to be always on the go. Sometimes it seems as if you just don't care how much money you waste on gas. explained Gio.

"Having her around meant a kind of a party, a revolution!" commented on of her friends. Although most of her sisters and brother were living near each other, it was she who would bring them together everytime she made her appearance in Etobicoke. She was the life of the party or the one organising something or other. Noise and laughter was a sign, that she was around.

Getting her family to do the craziest of things, together, She somehow convinced them, by literally dragging them from their houses and taking them for long walks. So she choose that autumn day. Up as usual, early in the morning when the sun was just beginning to filter though the trees, casting a great light of colours, she decided that, that was the day to wake up her family and get them together for a very special walk.

The nip in the air got them all into tracksuits and they went skipping and jumping to the nearest park. The trees seemed to be attuned, dancing with the Autumn winds showering everyone with leaves that had turned from green to yellow, orange, golden browns and to finally to burgandy - this great variety of hues. All seen at the same time. Sometimes there was such a blaze of colour that looked as if the forest was set on fire. All the sisters, brothers, nieces and nephews, got together and began collecting the leaves and making big, big heaps of leaves and then showering each other.

Everyone danced or began prancing around just like children without a care in the world, trying to be the one who showered the others with the greatest amount of leaves. They were all hail and hearty and when they finally arrived at Patricia's house, everyone were really hungry. Generally everyone pooled in by bringing something to eat and drink, so that's when they feasted on all the niceties that each one had brought.

Naturally everyone was hungry not only due to the walking but the sports they practised along the routes they had followed. Every couple of feet away there was a special exercise they could practise and this ran right through the whole park. So you can imagine how very tired they were at the end of it, but mentally revived.

Giovani, her husband was quite a serious man.... poles apart from his wife. He hated going out to theatre, cinema, festivals and didn't quite care for any type of gatherings. He was happy with pottering around his garden or building something around the house. But one thing the whole family enjoyed was open-air activities. So they not only went for long walks but often went mushroom picking. He taught the family how to distinguish between the poisonous and non-poisonous ones. The dog went along with them, usually running after the children and sometimes roughing out with them. He abors city life. They also enjoyd travelling a great deal from the East to the West without any problems, so they got to visit may cities in Europe, United States and Canada. Both he and his daughter drove across from the East to the West of Canada, on one occasion.

CHAPTER 24

MARIO POALO FELLINI

Mario Poalo Fellini was a debonair, young man. He was 5.10ft. brown-haired, with a slight wave. He had an athletic body. He not only broke all the hearts of women because of his looks but also due to his taking ways. A perfect ladies' man which proved that Chivalry hadn't died it' s death.- quite the ladies' man. But this didn't go to his head.

Surprisingly enough he wasn't married at the age of 30. This was an added attraction not only to single women but also to mothers whoe were on the hunt for a suitable partner for their single daughters. Well-to-do he moved about in a wealthy circle. Life here only added to his boredom and that's what kept him from getting caught. Contrary to his sophisticated look, he was easy to get aong with.

He had lived in a little village in the outskirts of Genova where his parents had a big farm which was run by two of his brothers. They also had a boutique called; "Milano". One of his sisters worked with his father there. The shop was comprised of two sections. "He / She".

This is one of the most elegant shops in the city. He gave a hand every time he was in town. The father so wanted him to take over the shop from him but Mario had other ideas.

No sooner had he finished his career in Mine Engineering, he decided to further his studies in Business Management on his father's insistence. But to his father's chagrin, he just left his father high and dry and joined one of the biggest companies that specialised in the importation of coal and the processing of this raw material. The manufactured products were sold to any East European countries and to the Asia.

He was not only intelligent but a hard worker. Having a knowledge of English, Spanish and Italian, it took him a long way. Most of his business trips took him to the United States His natural persuasive ways was an added characteristic that helped him enormously, as a salesman. His determination aided with the correct approach – not too pushy, took him a long way towards success. He spent three months a year travelling to the States.

But at Christmas time he usually took his vacations as his father required his presence in the Boutique. So frankly speaking it was far from relaxing, rather taxing, he would say. His father always harboured the idea that he would one day capture his son and make him take over the shop.

Knowing that this could be a rather tiring period for his father, and because he loved his father enormously, was one of he reasons why he had chosen to be home during this time.

His distinguished look sold their clothes as he was a walking exhibit of quality and elegance During the short moments he spent in the women's section he sold a great deal.

"You should be working here instead of trotting along the globe, working for somebody else, when you could be doing so for yourself!" His father often commented, hoping that it would rub off on him sometime or rather.

Women circulated false stories of a broken love affair because all the guile used by women seemed to have no effect on him. Some thought he was conceited, others threw themselves at him, all in vain. Off and on, he would go out with some of them but dropped them like hot cakes when he discovered how spoilt and empty some of them were. Seen in the company of many of these rich women it often seemed as if he were a Don Juan! He found their talk banal and empty and so lost interest in them.

"When are you going to settle down? I think your company kills you with work. You have no time for women. You should come home and find a nice girl here. Mr. Rossini and his wife have commented on that. Both the families could together control the fashion world and design. You have the qualities of a good salesman! Why don't you give it a serious thought.!"

His mother would not stop drumming into an otherwise deaf ear.

"Mum, everything has a time and place. I haven't found the right girl as yet and when I do, I will let you know. Don't worry, I am still young and handsome!"

Saying this he would bring a smile to his mum's eyes. They adored each other.

CHAPTER 25

GIOVANI IN VIRGINIA

It was a freezing wintry March in 1992, when the company sent him to the states on business. He had to travel to Virginia. He spent a hectic week wielding and dealing for the company. Everyday on the go meeting clients a string of clients, trying to wangle a decent deal for the company, back in Italy.

On this special trip one of his clients Tyran Rothschild invited him to a party.

"Mario what are you doing this Saturday? I know you will not be leaving for yet another week Tyran was a calm, friendly person and this had been the fourth time he had met him. Why don't you come over to my place for a small party?"

"Well, that's just wonderful! It would be a pleasure. But do you think, I would be comfortable. Everyone there will be a stranger to me, so that makes me a wee bit nervous."

"Please don't worry, I am sure you are going to feel very comfortable, with us, so please do come. It would do you a world of good and this would be an introduction to the real American world. You people in Europe think that we spend boring lives, enclosed in winter, at home."

"Now we are not going to talk shop. I am sure, that after the party, maybe you would work better tomorrow, as you will get to think like the Americans, but make sure you don't drink too much."

"Now If I were you I'd be careful and not be signing any papers, tomorrow! Take a day off and relax, you've been working way too much. I'd rather you had a sleep after the late night party. I'm afraid if not, I may be tempted to take you for a ride as I shall be in a bad humour if you woke me up early to do business.

"You've just convinced me not to go to your party. So thank you, but "NO", not under those conditions" said Mario seriously

Tyran's face fell. "Maybe your command of English is not good enough! But I was just teasing.

"I was told that there is a proverb that says, "Many a true word is said in a jest!" said Mario.

"But who cares!" He added after he saw a shadow cross Tyran's face.

"Eh! Got you!"

They took to each other, the very first time they met. But this didn't keep them from continually fencing each other. For the past few years they have been having many company dinners, together. During these years Tyran was about the only friendly person he got close to. But this had been the first time he was invited to their home for a party.

Tyran was married to Julia. Both were quite slim and tall. They were originally from Dallas, Texas. But due to his job, they had to leave their families back there. Tyran had been working for this company for the past ten years.

Julia used to work for the newspaper, there. Since coming here, she worked in one of the Graffic Designing Company. They had three children Janet 12, Jason 14, and Arleen 20. They were all still studying.

Janet and Jason were rather attractive. They resembled their mother in looks and height. While Arleen was walking image of her father. They each had their own character and were quite popular in sports. Jason was a good base –player player, while Arleen was a tennis player. Being a strong left hand player she had won many city championships.

On the contrary Janet only played for amusement. She hated competitions, neither did her parents force her to change her attitude. She was more a creative person and enjoyed sketching and painting. Often she got into trouble with her teachers when she was discovered doodling. Some teachers were under the mistaken idea that she used to be day-dreamer.

Before they parted Tyran said, "I'll pick you up at the hotel at 7pm."

Mario went to the hotel thinking of the party. Although he was curious about it, he was a bit uncomfortable

To begin with this would be the first time and he really didn't know how their parties went on nor did he know many people there. He was sure that Tyran and his wife would make sure that he was comfortable, so he thought, "Why, not? This is part of the adventure. I am going to make sure I enjoy myself.

It was Saturday and the day dawned bright and beautiful. He was filled with an excitement, he couldn't explain.

"Yes, I am looking forward to this party." But as the day went by and it was time for him to get dressed he was a bit nervous. So after a shave he got ready and decided to go down, to the lobby for a drink.

"Good evening sir, can I get you a drink?" asked the waiter with a smile.

"A gin and tonic, please" said Mario.

Mario looked round to observe the people who were busy chatting with their friends and colleagues.

One of them approached him, "You are not from here, sir! Where are you from?" "I am Samuel Rivers from London!"

Samuel was red-haired and very tall. He had a very cheerful face and seemed to be smiling all the time. Though when he laughed, he literally roared. He had a tummy which said that he drank a lot. He was very friendly.

"I am Mario Poala Fellini, from Italy. How are you?" They both shook hands and were soon on friendly terms, discussing their cultural differences.

"How do you like it here?"

"I find it very exciting. But it could be lonely, if you don't know anybody here."

"I've come here for a congress which comes to an end tomorrow, which is rather disappointing as I am just beginning to enjoy myself."

They spoke for about half an hour, promising to get in contact with each other if they do travel to each of their countries. They had hardly exchanged cards when Maro spied Ryan coming in through the lobby,

"I have to leave, it's been a great pleasure to have met you and have a safe trip, tomorrow.

They parted with a vigorous handshake.

"Oh don't you look dashing! I can see all the girls ignoring me this time."

He then led him to the garage, where he had parked his car.

Melani had gone to her nieces' wedding, in Chesapeake, Virginia. Chesapeake. to her was a city of contrasts, a pastoral paradise of parks, rivers and camp grounds. She was assured that the mies of sparkling beaches along its bay and the Atlantic Ocean would lure any beach lover from all over to this popular resort city ad that she was going to find it irresistible. This way we could convince you to visit us more often, hoping that it would hold you captive now that you are here. She was soon to discover that the beach was only the beginning. It went on to create a never–ending seaside Eden, complete with 18th century lighthouses, Colonial homes, and a Victorian – era life-saving station brimming with Marine Artifacts.

They took her to the new Marine Science Museum with a 50,000 gallon aquarium that replicates an under-sea "slice" of the bay. She realised that it must be a delightful, dilemma for sports lovers to have to make a choice between deepsea fishing and diving, canoeing, numerous other water sports and golf. Here there is a Beach Art Centre with special exhibits, galleries, classes and other activities. "I also had the opportunity of exploring the depths of a semi-tropical park.

Melani was just spending a fortnight at her sister's place and she felt fortunate to have had this great opportunity to leave her home. This was her favourite niece who thought it was indispensable that her favourite aunt attended her wedding. Her Husband Gio was a workaholic and could never find time to take some time off.

During her stay she was extremely busy with selecting clothes, wedding decorations, and helping her sister with all the arrangements from a to z. Everyone was extremely busy with last minute preparations. So by the end of the week she was pretty tired. It was just at this time, that her younger sister decided that it was time for her sister to have a complete change.

"Melani, one of our friends is having a party in their house and they have invited us, including you. Since I mentioned that you were in town they extracted a promise that we would bring you along. This will give you an opportunity to meet some of our good friends. Besides I think it's high time you made a little escape from all this confusion, here.

"Well, I am not sure. It has been ages since I have been to a party. I've forgotten how it is to be sociable!"

"I wouldn't like to get into the bad books with my friends. They are looking forward to meeting you, so there's no way out, now! You have been living quite the hermit's life and it's high time, we did something about it. I know that Gio hates to dance. So now you will have this great opportunity. Do you recall how much we used to all dance. Well we have to do once again, especially with the wedding, we will have to get you trained for the same." Yvonne, didn't wait for an answer, she took it for granted that she would go.

Not before she discussed it with Gio, who encouraged her to go. "Are you sure, I won't feel like a fish out of water?" asked Melani nervously.

The day dawned bright and beautiful. Yvonne rushed with Melani to keep their appointment at the hair-dressers. It was sunny but cool. It was the first days of spring. The excitement seemed to catch up with Melani and she wanted to look her best as the day before her sister cajoled her into buying something pretty for the party.

At around 7:15, "Come on ladies, stop titivating. It's time to leave."

No sooner than he heard them come down the stairs, he turned and gave out a whistle.

"Wow, aren't I lucky to be escorting two of the best dames in town! I can imagine the coveted looks I ma going to get. You both look gorgeous! With a twinkle in his eye, he said, "I really don't know who to choose!"

"Come on, let's go and make the guys envious!" With that Randy opened the car door and they were off to Ryan's house.

Randy rang the doorbell. Tyran opened the door and literally gaped. "Now who are these pretty ladies? Don't you have a beautiful sister-in law. Why have you been hiding her all these days? It's pretty clear we are going to have problems keeping the boys at bay, don't you agree Randy?"

"Welcome to Virginia Melani! How do you like it here, or have you had the opportunity of seeing anything?

I was told that you have been hibernating … too busy with the wedding, eh! I am very pleased you came and so will Marilyn." With that he called out to her.

She came toward them, with a tray in her hand.

"Hello Yvonne, I suppose this is your pretty sister! So they did convince you at last. As I was told that you weren't keen on coming. I would have been very disappointed if you hadn't. Maybe we would have gone and dragged you out of the house if you didn't come!"

With that she ushered them into a cheerful, spacious living room. Some of her friends were already there.

"Charmaine, this is Yvonne's sister Melani, from Ontario Canada. Soon everyone was offered a drink

A moment later Ryan said, "There's someone I would like you to meet, very specially. He is from Italy and I was told that your husband is from Italy, too. So may be you would make this young man feel comfortable speaking his language as he is tired of having spoken English all these days. So do allow his brain a rest."

"Mario, this lady speaks a couple of Latin Languages, so I thought this would help you communicate better.

He usually teased him a great deal.

.... ITALIAN SENTENCES

He had a kind of magnetism, in his eyes that seemed to hold hers, much against her wishes, just for a fleeting second. But to her it seemed a long, moment! It was electrifying! She felt uncomfortable under his penetrating look. Though his handshake was firm but comforting. She took in his appearance. He looked outstanding here because he was tanned and very handsome. You could clearly see that he was a foreigner.

"I am so relieved to meet someone who can speak the same language as I do! I had to do so much of wielding and dealing these days that I am dead beat. Italian expressions ....

She soon discovered that he was very fluent in English. They conversed for a few moments until Charmaine came over to introduce them to some of her friends.

"I was wondering where you have been hiding. I add that Ryan and I are very that there is someone who is helping to make our special guest Mario comfortable."

Soon the men got together in groups as usual often talking shop while the women folk on the other hand exchanged gossip of all that had been happening in town. It was evident that they hardly met as everyone was extremely busy. On the whole they were quite a friendly bunch so Melani soon lost her shyness and felt very much at home in their company.

After having passed some snacks around, they put some music on. Some couple were on the floor. Melani sensed that Randy and Yvonne wanted to dance, so she said, "Why don't you guys go ahead and dance, I shall be fine. Don't let me keep you from enjoying yourself because I know you love to dance."

They were hardly on the floor when, Excuse me, would you like to dance, if you could tolerate my walking on your toes." He said this looking her straight in the eye. She turned away to cover her confusion. He was quite the entertainer.

Yvonne and Randy approached them, "Are you having a good time?"

Mario said, "Thanks to your sister-in-law, she is quite the entertainer!" He said with a twinkle in his eye.

As they passed them Randy said to his wife, "It seems as if they are made for each other. Is your sister happy with her husband?"

"Well, I haven't heard otherwise. Not that she ever complains about anything. She had always been that way. I feel that they are happily married.

"What do you usually do? How long have you been here?" He plied her with questions as his curiosity was aroused the moment he set eyes on her.

"Well I am a housewife and I also work in the weekends."

"So you really have no time to be naughty. I was told that you are married. I feel that your husband is a very lucky man, that's why he never complains about you keeping as busy as you do.!

He went on to explain that he was from Genoa, a coastal town in the North of Italy. I've only been here for a week, on business.

"Do you work in the same company as Randy?" questioned Melani.

"No, our company does business with them, that's how I came to know Ryan. He works in the same department as I do. We are both in the Marketing Department. My company works with Chemicals. We import coal from here."

"You live in Canada, don't you? I was told that it is very beautiful. It's a pity we don't have any business there, but I would like to visit. I am crazy about fresh-water fishing, it's one of my most important hobbies, so I am hoping to do that in Canada. You have very big lakes and rivers. But I wouldn't like to live there as it could be extremely cold. Is it true that it's so chill there sometimes, especially with the corridor winds that icicles could literally form under your nose. No, I prefer to be in my country where the temperatures don't go as low as that or rather nothing near that. Maybe I'll go there, next summer! If you'll be my guide," he added playfully.

"Oh, sure it would be a pleasure for both my husband and I to show you around," She said mischievously. He winced a little when she mentioned her husband. He didn't quite like that!

"So I suppose you are married. Do you have any children?"

"Yes, my husband is from Italy, too. We have two children a boy and a girl.

My husband is also from Genoa, maybe you know him. He works in a construction company and also works for an Italian company. They generally do all the tiling and marble in Canada. This is one of the busiest times of the year for him and that's why he couldn't come." She readily found an excuse for her husband's absence.

"If I were your husband, I wouldn't let you out of my sight!" He said teasingly. Melani blushed and lowered her eyes so he wouldn't see her reaction.

"Etobicoke is on the outskirts of Toronto, yet easy to commute there. It's quite peaceful there, most of the people live in houses with the exception of some town houses and a couple of skyscrapers. We have all the amenities within reach. We are well communicated. There are buses and trains on a very regular basis. Especially at peak hours they run every couple of minutes. There are slow and fast trains. It just take about half an hour to go the greatest of distances. It takes less that 15 minutes to go down town, to Toronto. We have a beautiful park, tennis courts, swimming pools and places for children to play and fields for base-ball and whatever."

"You love the city I can see it. So a visit is a must!"

"Well how long have you come here for?" questioned Melani.

"I have actually come to the end of my stay here. I didn't realise that I was going to feel so nostalgic about leaving here. I usually look forward to going home, but this time it seems as if something is holding me back.

Both of them were getting on tremendously that they didn't realise the fight of time. Dinner was served and they were placed near each other.

"Should you visit Italy, don't forget to contact me." He said, giving her his card.

"It has given me enormous pleasure to have spoken to you and I hope that this is not going to be the last time we see each other!" The magic of that moment was broken as Ryan came over.

"I hope the two of you have enjoyed our party. Mario, what about you, what do you think about our parties?

I guess this is the first time you have been to one and I hope it is not going to be the last.

Now would you say tht American life is boring? Isn't that a misconception?"

"Well I've had an unforgettable time, thanks to you.

"I am glad to hear that!" as he walked away from them.

"I can't imagine that tomorrow, rather in a coupe of hours I shall be on my way, back to Italy. I never, ever thought that the USA would hold such a great attraction for me." His voice broke as he continued. All the time his eyes dwelling on Melani.

"I wish I had met you before. As much as I hate to leave now, there's no way out. When are you leaving?"

"In a week's time. Frankly speaking I hadn't been keen on coming to this party but my sister insisted. And I am glad I did." she said hesitatingly.

"Do you often come here? I'd love to meet you again."

"The way he said it, made my heart skip a beat!" she thought

"Does that sound impossible to you?" he continued when he saw that look of surprise on her face.

"You know I don't believe that anything is impossible, at least it doesn't exist in my vocabulary. I am sure that we are going to meet again, at least that's what my intuition says. This party has been and will be an unforgettable experience. Thanks to you I had a wonderful time. What about you?" She gave a shy smile and didn't answer him.

"I'm going to give you my address and telephone number, in Italy. Even though I travel a lot, I always receive my mail. So don't forget to keep in contact. Would you be in Genova soon? If so, do let me know!" With that he gave her a light kiss on her face and gave her out-stretched hand, a squeeze"

"I felt his body shiver as he did so...I was filled with a fatality so great, that I thought I wouldn't be able to handle this situation. I turned and he was gone".

All this seemed quite ridiculous to her. She pinched herself to make sure that she was awake. "Why would something like this happen to me? Am I crazy? Have I forgotten that I am a married lady with two wonderful children?" She then rushed this aside as she thought, "You crazy cout, this is only a transient part of life."

"This couldn't have been happening to me! What's wrong with you?" I kept asking myself "Now this isn't me- the prude. I've only been with this guy for a few hours and what an impact he has made on me? I haven't drunk to much, have I? I hardly drink. Is it because I did have some today?...No way! That's impossible! I'm not drunk! Why am I filled with such a great excitement that seem to be bitter-sweet- more bitter! He just left and I already began to miss him. Relax, you're just smitten by this flashy guy, who has turned you on. Don't worry, you'll soon forget him after all you've only been speaking to him this evening."

All these questions ran through her brain and seemed to cause a turmult within she felt she couldn't control. "This is not me!" She enphasized. Family life to her was the second most important priority after God.

She was soon to discover that this feeling was not going to disappear, it was going to haunt her incessantly in the coming months, in spite of giving her time and ever being so busy. "This is just crazy. No words uttered nothing, nothing to pointedly give one, a rational reason why this could had happen to anyone- no – to either of us, because I strongly felt that that evening was going to change our lives in one way or another. She smiled sadly as she contemplated her situation.

"I am married and have a pretty established life. What's wrong with me? Naturally he must have been very lonely and that's why he was patronising me. Secondly, this is very silly on my part to give him a second thought. There's no way anything could have happen to us! In normal circumstances things like these never happen to people like me. Maybe he was just being polite I had a strong feeling that I Must have caused a reaction on him. There was a something a sudden spark that seems to burn inside me, I have never felt something like this since I met my husband Giovani. He was part and parcel of my life."

She was filled with awe as she was suddenly brought back to Earth with a bump, when Yvonne shouted, "Hey! Where the hell are you? Are you deaf? Are you alright?"

I realised that I was letting myself get carried away with all those silly ideas of mine, it seems as if I am a naïve teenager. I'd better cut it all out" as these thoughts ran through her head.

Neither of us have done anything wrong, nor have we even said a word to express any feelings but it all seemed like a traitor playing tricks with two innocent people, I had a strong perception that the feeling that run through my head was mutual. There was no way of knowing his present reaction…

He confirmed this when, the next day he couldn't resist waking her up at six AM in the morning, "I'm sorry, I know that I'm disturbing you but I needed to hear your voice just one more time before I left, I'm at the airport at this moment, in half an hour time I must be boarding the airplane. It was wonderful to have met you, and it's not going to be the last time", he stammered as he spoke.

He couldn't put any more, into words, I knew he was still on the phone, neither could I say anything except "Yes, that was a greaaat party", as her voice broke, "Have.. a safe trip" I said, trying to make it final, "Bye!"

"Thanks for such an unforgettable time, don't lose my card. Bye!" with hat he hung up.

I turned pale, I felt sick in my stomach, I ran to the bath and burst into tears. Luckily everyone was asleep and that I happened to be near the phone when it rung. The sickening feeling revealed the truth, "You're in love!"

"No," I told myself, "this could only be a Fata Morgana! A mirage! There was no way out. Oh yes, there is, this is just a passing infatuation that would ease in time, all I had to do was to put it in its right perspective and I realised that it was all just a figment of my imagination. Come down to earth- be realistic!" that's what I kept telling myself.

The next few days were as if, in her words, "I just walked around in a dream, yes, that's exactly what I felt, I could see him everywhere,

I tried to oust him out of my brain, but the more I tried, all the more I pictured him everywhere. At times I had to bounce back to earth when I was told: Where are you? Are you ill? Is something wrong with you?" often this was a complaint from everyone around. So she decided to bry herself to complete dedication to her niece's wedding.

"Don't you think you re taking over to many responsibilities on your shoulders? Why don't you make the others do their part too?" he won't kept repeatedly saying "common, let's go out and do some sight-seeing. You haven't seen the city, so let's try to change that." Ad that's exactly what her sister did. They titivated a bit and were soon out of the house on their way to the city.

"I convinced you to come here because I thought you needed a break, but now I find that you're killing yourself Don't you think you have been working enough?" she was determined to make her sister enjoy this trip with that they got into the car and were off.

CHAPTER 26

VIRGINIA

Virginia was regarded as the gateway to the south because it occupies the middle position on the Atlantic seaboard of the United States. It was named after Queen Elizabeth I, England's "Virgin Queen" is also known as the mother of presidents because it's the birth place of eight US presidents. George Washington, Thomas Jefferson, James Madison, James Monroe, William Henry Harrison, John Tyler, Zackery Taylor and Woodrow Wilson. The tour guide carried on giving details as they were shown around the city. Yvonne thought that that was the best way to get to know and see the city.

The state forms a rough triangle, with North Carolina and Tennessee to the South, Maryland, Chesapeake Bay, and the Atlantic Ocean to the North East and East and West Virginia and Kentucky to the North West and West. Virginia played a pivotal role in the American revolution and the civil war, some of its remains could be still seen. The continued in the coach and drove around.

The resident population in Virginia is over seven million-1992- and more of half of them live in the crescent-shape urban corridor that stretches from Arlington and Alexandria in the North through Friedricksburg, the state capital Richmond, and Petersburg, to Newport, Hampton, Portsmouth and Northfolk. The cities of Charlottesville, Lynchsburg and Roanok lie to the West, the rapid inflats of the people to Northern Virginia has been great in the last twenty five years.

Fortunately the climate in Virginia was temperate unlike the intense heat in Ontario in summer. So one could walk around for hours without getting very tired, no doubt the humidity could sometimes become unvariable, but the rain helps to cool it down off and on. Two thirds of Virginia is covered with forests of pine, cypress and very hard woods.

Melany was static, when Yvonne invited her to a couple of musicals in Richmond, where the Virginia Museum of Fine Arts, which is the principal state-funded cultural facility in the state, presenting drama and music as well as arts exhibit. The three days they spent there were far too short for all that they wished to visit they also managed to see the private Valentin museum and the museum of Confederacy. In Norfolk, the Chrysler Museum and in Newport the Mariner's Museum. It also has many music and dance companies. They were surprised to find that Virginia had a number of orchestras. They were told that the Barter Theater in Abington has one national recognition as has the Federal funded Wolf Trap Farm Park for the performing Arts, part of the National Park System. What surprised melany most of all were not the local libraries, but the book mobiles, which she had never ever seen before.

A visit to Richmond took them to famous historic homes, specially George Washington's at Mount Vernon and Thomas Jefferson's at Monticello and the Colonial Settlements.

Since having met Mario, Melani's curiosity about coal grew. So she lapped tap all information she could get. She knew that Virginia had large resources of bituminious coal and small quantities of petroleum and natural gas. So coal and timber were the most valuable industries there. The coal-fields are found mainly in the Apalachian mountains area.

"Don't you think we've had enough of this crap?" asked Yvonne, who had not been particularly keen on having spent so much of their time with this group of tourists. But Melany seemed to be enjoying every moment of it because she had decided to learn all she could of this city, and was the one who had convinced Yvonne to go on this guided tour, when she discovered that Yvonne had little or no interest nor knowledge f anything of the historical past of the city.

On the contrary, Yvonne could not understand why Melani had such interest for such topic which to her were terribly boring. Since having met Mario, Melani's interest for the city had become of primary importance to her. She knew that it was now or never.

That night, when they returned to the hotel, Yvonne was so tired that she went to bed, but Melani lay in bed and tried as she might, she couldn't sleep, instead she recalled all these moments she spent in conversation with Mario. The Chemical Company in which Mario worked, bought all the supply of coal from here. She realised that she would never had been so interested in such a subject.

Yvonne became a wee bit suspicious when she observed her sister's aspect. She thought there was some kind of change taking place n her which she had never seen before. She looked radiant.

"I have a strong feeling, that, that guy you met at the party has made a great impact on you. Am I right? If so, you must be completely out of your mind to allow someone you just met from nowhere to carry you off your feet! This is so ridiculous. I just finded hard to believe that a person as sensible as you are could have in such a foolish manner! It seems as if you are a fledgling about to bat its wings and fly into a world of adventure. I don't know if you've realised that there's been a change in you, for the better. I'm happy for you in a way, but at the same time I feel that your only going to get terribly hurt. If I were you, I'd bounce back to the real world. I guess in time you will, but I hope it won't be too late!"

Melani did realise that her sister was only trying to be of help but how could one explain such situations? Since his departure, she wanted to acquire all the knowledge she could on the subject of coal, which she thought, was just a means of getting to know him more, to feel that she was still beside him. She became well burst on that subject. She now recalled when he spoke to her, about the coal industry and everything that surrounded him. Although Mario was much more interested in getting to know more about her she wouldn't give him a chance, instead she plied him with numerous questions, just to cover her feelings at that moment. She thought this would keep him to busy to realise what had been happening to her. So he decided that just being with her was gratifying enough, even if it meant that he had to talk short with her, as he sort of seemed afraid of losing her at that moment.

She kept recalling all the conversation they have had. "Do you know all the numerous problems that miners in Europe have to face?

Recently I read about the numerous accidents that take the lives of miners in a little province in the North of Spain called Asturias. You must have heard of what had happened there. Well, according to the results of the investigations it has proved that most accidents were caused by human errors" he added.

"I think the fatal conditions of the mines they have been working in, due to the profound depth the miners had to go and with methods that were very risky, maybe still using conventional method, using cutters, chain saws mobile or hand-held electric or hydraulic drills. In such situations the holes were loaded with explosives or other breaking methods that dislodge the coal from the seam. Often they were faced with sudden explosions caused by bags of methane gas found during the process of digging. That usually resulted in causing the walls to cave in, thus burying the miners, who often founded just impossible to escape. At times there were miners who irresponsibly even attempted to go into the mine with a tad too much of alcohol."

[Strange as it may seem in this day and age, the same province and the same mine has hit the headlines in the newspapers of the whole world as a group of completely irresponsible miners sold dynamite to a group of people that happened to be terrorists, the ones who blew up some trains, the sadly remembered 3/11 in Madrid. Over CHECK INFORMATION FROM NEWSPAPER-NUMBER OF DEAD PEOPLE people died and over NUMBER OF WOUNDED were wounded]

"Why do people still continue to work, when they know that there's such a high percent of risk involved in the job?" Melani asked.

"Well, to begin with, they are highly paid. Secondly, they have been used to the idea. Most of the families have had the experience of their past generations working at it" explained Mario. "This makes them forget that everytime they go down, they have a clear idea of what they have to face. And as always, this becomes a habit. What do you think of climbers who just scale the most difficult and dangerous walls- just for the insulin that flows through their bodies, creating a great excitement within them? No doubt a miner's job isn't as exciting as that, well, there wouldn't be any excitement at all, but it's a way of life."

"For a moment I was so immersed in it that I nearly forgot where we were. It seemed as if it were just the two of us" said Melani. That had been when Rhyan had come rushing towards us. "So there you are! We were wondering whether you were lost or maybe up to tricks. Now Mairo, how did you manage to keep Melani so engrossed? Did I hear right? You weren't teaching her all about coal, were you?" "No, you'd be very surprised how much she knows about the subject"

"Have you lost your head? Is that all you could talk about? I have never met her before and you've been petronising her, without having given any of us, an opportunity of talking to her at all." grumbled Rhyan.

"Now, don't tell me that Yvonne dragged Melani out of the house much against her will just to come here and be entertained with the subject of coal."

With that they were brought back to civilisation

Melani got to learn that Mario worked in the industry that imported coal and used it, in the production of coal tar and coke and other derivatives. This is what brought him another salesman from the company often to Virginia, where the most extensive and important deposits of coal are found in North America. US has approximately 31% of the known recoverable coal reserves in the world.

She soon learned that in modern mining, access to underground mines was gained by three primary methods. In the Drift Mine Method, the seam of the coal is exposed to the surface on the side of a hill or mountain, and the mine opening is made directly into the coal seam. This is generally the easiest and the least expensive way to open an underground coal mine. In the Slope Mine Method, an inclined opening through rock strater is used to gain access to the coal seam. If the coal seam itself is inclined, the slope may follow the seam. Slope Mine Access is usually used where less overburden is present. In the Mine Shaft Method, the coal seam is reached by a vertical opening from the surface. Combinations of access methods may be used depending on conditioners of the coal seams.

Once access is gained to the coal bed, three primary mining systems are used in the United States, classified according to the equipment used, they are the Conventional, Continuers and Long-Wall Methods.

CHAPTER 27

NEW LIFE

Melani returned home a different person, no doubt the change was wonderful. Giovani and the kids were at the airport to meet her.

"You look very well. I can see that the holiday has done you good." said Giovani.

"Your haircut looks very sophisticated and on the whole, you look lovely mum" joined both the teenagers who seemed to have grown up.

Little they have realised that she had fallen in love!

She had taken loads of gifts for everyone, it didn't take both Pete and Kody long to find their gifts- mostly clothes and other little presents sent to them by their cousins, aunt and uncle. She bought Gio a very expensive and beautiful Omega watch. He kept examining it and completely forgot to thank her for it- very typical of him. He didn't believe in trivialities nor was he demonstrative about such things. But it was clear that he liked it. As she walked around the house, she founded spic and span.

"Now this is a wonderful surprise! Yes I can see that, you have all done a great job. Have you missed me? Or have you been up to tricks while I was away?" asked Melani.

"Mum, we were rather busy preparing for our exams, but dad, must have been a bit bored, because he used to do the cleaning a lot more than we have seen while you were away. Yes, he also took us to the Chinese restaurant a couple of times, he also ordered our favourite pizza one day. I guess he didn't enjoy cooking while you were away!"

Back home Melani decided that try as much as she could to forget Mario, he seemed to keep haunting her constantly. Often she was so lost in thought that one day she nearly caused a fire. If she wasn't brought back to Earth with the strong burnt smell of the food. This is when she decided she had to do something to change her life. After a short period of analizing, she realised that the best bet was to go back to University, so she applied to York University.

A week later Pete called out. "Guess what mum? You've received a letter from York University? Did you write to them? You must know that we still ave a couple of years before we go there, so don't you think it is to early to do something about it now?"

Melani's eyes lit up with great expectation. "Now let me see that letter" she asked.

All the three pairs of eyes were fixed on her face as she opened the letter and read its contents. She broke into a smile as she said, "Guess what? I've actually been admitted into the University! I didn't tell you anything abut it because I wasn't sure they would accept me! Don't you think this is a great idea?"

For a moment Gio seemed to be perplexed and Pete looked crestfallen with the exception of Kody who excitedly said: "Congratulations mom! I'm glad for you! That's great. It's high time you did something to change your life and make it more interesting. This is one way you'll break out of your routine and get to learn a great deal and also keeo active. Besides, you're going to get the great opportunity of meeting a lot of people and not just staying all alone at home, while we are all away most of the day."

"Now what about the cooking and cleaning?- the house has a hole" interrupted Pete.

"Haven't we managed to do so while she was away? Well, we could continue doing so. Everyone can contribute towards doing all the work, can't we? Aren't we all adults?" insisted Kody.

A few more moments of discussion and they all agreed that it was a great idea. During the course of the day they all had numerous stories to share that she had not a moment to give way to her excitement about going back to University.

That night, in spite of being tired, she just couldn't sleep. Pictures of all that she expected to happen went through her brain. Yes, she would have to make a great deal of adjustment.

"I wonder what kind of companions I'm going to have, I bet they are all going to be younger and smarter than I am. After all, I haven't been studying for such a long time. But this, I knew was not going to be a problem. I was determined to do my best, I always read a great deal, so why can't I study too?" said Melani. She had a lot of literature in the house. During her spare time in the past, she used to grab moments to spend at the nearby library. Secondly she enjoyed following talk shows and watching documentals on TV.

She had to go to University for more detailed information. Classes weren't going to begin until the first week of September. There was ample time for her to prepare herself, but she was determined to visit University that very week.

On Thursday morning, she woke up bright and early and left the house after the rest of the family had done so. The previous day she had prepared the meals so that she would have the whole day to herself. It would take her about three hours back and forth to University, this one was one of the snags of having to live in Oakville. Although there was transportation, it was as quick as that of Etobicoke, where you have a constant flow of buses every five to ten minutes to downtown Toronto. Living on the outskirts of Oakville meant the bus came along every thirty to forty minutes depending on the part of the day. This took you to the railway station, where you caught the train. In winter it was pretty dangerous to drive sch a long way which would only create problems. Most of the people only drove t the station, where they left their cars and took the train which was so very comfortable.

Now this was the most romantic par of living in Oakville. This was no just ordinary train. It was unique. Very spacious compartments with great big windows that gave you the pleasure of seeing the very beautiful changing scenery of picturesque landscapes. Every time the train approached the station, you could hear the very special chime of the bell- an unusual, beautiful sounds that seemed to take you back to those good ol' trains of long ago that went chugging through the newly laid railway lines. At peak hours it could get packed. Most of the people didn't take their cars, because it was cheaper, less dangerous and more comfortable to take the train.

The train took the passengers directly to Union Station in Toronto, from where you could get a constant flow of trains going East, West,

North bound and South bound. There are a couple of coffee shops, bakeries where you could pick up the most delicious beef- patties to a great variety of donuts- most of them fruit-filled or with jellies to suit all tastes. There were newspaper stands and lottery centers. So there was no time to get bored while you waited for trains.

From Union Station she had to get two buses before she was dropped right inside the University Campus. A flight of steps took her to the lobby and the section for registration and information. After having checked her papers, "Ma'am, if you turn right you'll see a sign that says: Counselors, go in there and ask for Mr. Riley"

Once shown in, she had to wait for a few moments until he was free to attend to her.

"Good morning Mrs. Fellini, come on in. How are you today?"

"Good morning Mr. Riley. Well, to be sincere, I'm excited and nervous at the same time. I can hardly wait to attend classes once again, but I am a bit worried that I would be the only old student here and maybe I wouldn't be able to keep up with the rest of the younger students."

"Now, that should be the least of your worries. You can count on us to help you, and we have tutors too. They are at your disposal, at any time you require their help. We also have a huge library, that you can use. Feel free not only to consult books- but also to study here. Hmm.. I see you live in Oakville. You don't have to carry all your books up and down. No one would disturb you in the library- there's always perfect silence there! And since we've already had our discussion, I'll show you around"

With that they were soon engrossed in the necessary paperwork.

"We went through all the programs that were being offered in Law" said Melani.

Mr. Riley interrupted her "You must know that our University is well known for our specialisation on Law. There's no doubt that you'd have to do a great deal of studying. Secondly we don't tolerate tardiness nor absence. You could only be absent for a period of two days maximum, unless you bring us a doctor's certificate and that we'd require that you skip the term and then return the following semester, should you fall ill and you would not lose your fees. If otherwise your Tuition fees won't be returned, after the grace period of two days."

"The lecturers have chalked out periods of time where you could freely approach them if you need to clarify anything. Yes, we also have a section of videos, at the disposal of the students on real cases that took place in the past few years. So you see all we ask is just your will to do your best… the rest you can count on us for all other help you need. If you have a financial problem and require money for your education, you can also count on us. You'd have to fill in a form and we'll process it for you, free of charge. Now this usually takes time, so be prepared with part of the money which would cover for, the first term." Mr. Riley carried on, making sure that Melani was given all the information she required.

This was a huge modern university made of concrete. This gave it an ugly look unlike the University of Toronto, which had a character of its own. But this university although different, had everything you required. They had a block for residential students. On the whole this was practically new, just a few years old, so they had all the modern comforts one could foresee or expect.

CHAPTER 28

LIFE AT UNIVERSITY

Soon the day Melani was preparing for dawned. She woke up early and prepared breakfast for the family. She was filled with an exhilaration with just the thought of attending her first day of class. She had chosen the evening session. In this way she would have time not only to make sure that the family was not sacrificed due to one of her whims, but also will have time to handle her daily homework. She decided that she was going to do all in her power, to keep the family happy.

Now this was easily said than done. At first she found it difficult to handle, cooking, cleaning and studies all at the same time. Yes, she had a great deal of homework to be done that just couldn't be neglected. Fortunately the very first day they were given a course on Time Management. So within the first week, she made a schedule. She organised her time in such a way that she didn't get into, "one hell of a rut" which most of her sisters predicted.

She had to make drastic changes in her life and so did the family. They weren't prepared for this as much as they had all promised. So she had to make slow but steady changes in their lives – much more in her life though! At times she found herself getting into tenter hooks, finding it difficult to allocate time for studying. This was when she realised that she would have to burn the midnight candle. This in time became a habit and the family soon adjusted their habits accordingly. They did their very best not to disturb her when they woke up. No doubt they had had everything laid out on the table for breakfast. Yes, the kids now teenagers and even Gio accepted the idea and became more comprehensive. He gave the impression that he was pretty impressed with all that she had been doing. Everyone took turns to do all that was necessary and soon things began to run smoothly.

The students on the whole were mostly independent, young and unmarried. Now and again the teacher got the students to do group work. Some students were pretty co-operative and found that this created an incentive to work harder. Others preferred to work independently as their working hours didn't coincide. This wonderful ambience helped the students to score more than average marks. The teacher not only did that, but she also requested students who followed special routes, to give those who had no cars a lift to the nearest subway or bus stops, as classes ended pretty late. It was supposed to end at ten but quite often it went on until half –ten. So this was a great detriment rather than a help for people like me who lived more than 30 kms. away, from Toronto.

That's when Melani and Sharon got to become great friends. They often went to the University library to work together. This is where they did their major assignments, so they didn't have to carry library books home. Besides their quality of work also improved. They tried to work on a regular basis.

Sharon lived down town, but went out of her way to make sure that she dropped Melani, in a safe train station, considering the lateness of the hour! This at first was a very comfortable arrangement. It not only made things easy for her but also helped her catch an earlier train than if she had taken the bus. The first couple of months went smoothly. But soon it was late fall, the days began to grow shorter and gradually gave way to the freezing, cold wintry weather.

It was the 6th. Of December when they got their first heavy snowfall. Being inside the building they were completely unaware of the changing scenery outside which was to take everyone by surprise.

To Melani's misfortune Sharon didn't come to class that day. So she had to take the bus. To make matters worse she was far from familiar with this route. Sharon always made sure to drop her at the most suitable subway, where she would arrive home as fast as possible. Melani realised too late, that she should have been more independent and studied all the alternative routes.

Little did she realise what she was in for! So after class, on leaving the University she rushed around looking for the bus, for the first time, to take her to the subway. Needless to say everything looked far from familiar. This sudden, first heavy snowfall took everyone by surprise, especially considering the walls of snow that had soon infiltrated the whole area in such a short space of time. To make matters worse there was a thick fog. The whole scenery could have been considered beautiful during the day but at this ungodly hour, she felt completely disgruntled and awfully worried.

On arriving at the subway she must have got off the bus at the wrong stop. Although she could see the lights of the station she didn't realise that she had to walk a few yards away to arrive at the main entrance. Instead she walked toward the nearest doorway. The snow was pretty high, so with great difficulty, she ploughed through the snow, finally getting there.

Much to her disappointment she surprisingly discovered not a soul was there. Naturally she thought, what could one expect at this hour. Nervously she fumbled in her bag looking for her token. When she finally found one, she looked for the machine with the slot and found it.

"At first I was perplexed, but it soon turned to dismay when I finally found the machine and dropped the token that went through. But, no, it must have got stuck or so I had thought. The barrier wouldn't open. Through the glass door I could see a number of people moving around. But naturally they couldn't see me as they had, their back toward me.

Everyone seemed to be in such a hurry to get home. But one of the guys sitting at the counter could, but he wouldn't budge although I make signs, and kept banging the door expressing that I couldn't go in. He made a few gestures, I couldn't understand and continued controlling the passengers and selling them tickets. I guess he was too comfortable and warm, to bother to get up and come to me, or maybe, he thought that he had explained what I had to do. There was a distance from where he was sitting. I continued banging the door. Naturally nobody could hear me through those double-glazed, heavy thick doors.

Ten long minutes, that seemed like hours, went by and I thought of going back the way I had come but it was just impossible. The snow had not only covered my tracks but also formed a great big wall around. There was just no way I could do anything, unless I wished to get buried in there!"

"I began to panic! The ten minutes grew to twenty. I felt caged in. Being asthmatic, only made matters worse, I began to get claustrophobic."

Just at that moment a dark-skinned lady suddenly turned to look my way. Yes God was on my side and seemed to be taking care of me. I tried to explain my predicament. She approached the door and explained that the machine only accepted tickets. When I explained that I hadn't any, she very sweetly, passed one from under the door. Lo and behold the door opened and I was in. I thanked her profusely but she brushed me aside and wouldn't even accept the money for the ticket.

"Don't forget," she admonished "never to leave the house without both the tokens and the tickets because there are a few places that only one of them would be accepted. I know this shouldn't be, but that's the way the system worked, forgetting people who would fall into such a hapless condition you had been, in."

I closed my eyes and said a prayer of thanks and continued on my way.

I was mad with the ticket salesman and should have put in a formal complaint. But instead I soon forgot my precarious situation, instead of having thought of preventing others from falling into the same predicament, I had gone through. All I did was to pray that no one would fall into the same situation.

That's when I realised how much Sharon had spoilt me. She used to take me a longer distance than was necessary so that I would get home as early as possible. She made sure to take me right to the front door and never left until she made sure I had gone through, without a problem. This made me forget that there is such thing as - unforeseen circumstances - which at times could lead one to unpleasant situations when one reaches that comfort zone!

Fortunately she recalled the classes she had, had at the Broadcasting Centre where she was taught breathing exercises, that helped relieve the tension she was experiencing. So the moment she found a place in the train that's exactly what she did. If she hadn't done so she would have broken into a hysteria.

When she arrived home, she was completely dead beat. It was nearing midnight.

The family jumped the moment they heard the door open, as they were all in tenter hooks, worrying about her. Seeing her expression, Kodi immediately put some tea on for her, while Pete and Gio wanted know what had happened to her.

Gio's immediate re-action, "I think you should quit classes. It isn't worth all the trouble you are going through. I don't want you to end up getting ill.!"

But she was adamant, "As much as I realise how easy it is to do so, I'd rather continue. I accept this as part of life! I am fine now and I am sure after I have had, a good sleep, I shall be my old self."

"I think all of us need to sleep now." After a shower and a light dinner, she was dead to world.

That was not going to be the only scary experience she had to go through. First of all, just having to travel at that part of the day it wasn't unusual to see very strange characters, hovering around. She had been warned to always find a compartment where there were many people.

At times, although I kept telling myself that, "all this is part of life!" My instincts seem to disagree with me.

"You should have priorities, but one has to make sure that those priorities shouldn't clash with the harsh realities of life!"

"Do I need to go through all this? What purpose does this serve? Isn't just going to the gym sufficient or maybe just Yoga tha helps one to relax!"

"No she seems to have the happy knack of going the hard way!" Said her sisters. So she continued going to classes.

Little did she realise that this didn't end there. She was in for another nightmare.

It must have been the fourth time that she had taken the bus from the station, to the house. There were two that ran the same route but one dropped her at her doorstep and the other in a street parallel to it. To one who isn't very familiar, all the streets looked the same. But when the scenery changes, it only adds to one's confusion.

Always in a hurry to get home, she hopped into the first bus that she found.

Now that wasn't a normal day! It was, dark and very foggy, with heavy snow falling, all around. You could scarely see a yard from where you were. Even the bravest of hearts wouldn't be comfortable in this mysterious scary night where not a soul, nor a car could be seen.

When she arrived at the supposed-to- be door, of her house and the automatic lights came on, she became aware that she wasn't in her home. At the entrance to her home a cluster of pines, lined her drive.

She had given the bus driver her address and he assured her that she would have no problem as her house was just around the corner. This of course was far from true. So she decided to look around, but all she found was a huge curtain in front of her. As she went from one street to another it dawned her that she was walking in circles. She seemed to have no sense of direction whatsoever. To top it all she began to get jittery. But finally common sense took over and she decided to give her husband a call.

Now where could she call him from? There were hardly any lights on. So she approached the first one she came across. She rang the door-bell. Now people are very wary and don't usually open their doors to people at night, much less on a night like that! But since she kept insisting, the lady finally opened the door.

She was extremely rude.

"What are you doing here, at this time of the night, especially on a night like this?"

She was about to bang the door on her face when she tearfully begged. "Please mam, I've just come from the University, I had taken the wrong bus and now I am completely lost, may I call my husband to come and pick me, please?"

Seeing her books and realising that this girl was in real trouble, she let her in, and allowed her to make the call.

Frankly speaking this didn't help very much as she couldn't tell what street she was in, as all the names had been completely covered by snow. But the lady helpfully gave her address.

He told her that he'd be there as soon as he could. Five long, long…… minutes passed.

When things go wrong, they have the happy knack of getting so entangled that seems impossible to disentangle To make matters worse, she was so filled with panic that she couldn't keep her cool.

To add to it, being as impatient as she was, she began walking around, looking for the headlights of her husband's car. No car could be seen, so she decided to ring another door-bell.

Yes this entrance had very bright, inviting lights and the door seemed to be open. She was in luck's way! Thanking her stars she ran towards it, only to realise that a man was lying flat on the ground. Seeing that, she took to her feet as fast as her feet could carry her.

"Is this man dead? NO …no … she wanted to know nothing, about it. She took to her heels and nearly crashed into a car that had just come around the corner. Fortunately that car had good brakes and avoided crashing into her. Thank God, it was none other than her husband. Breathing hard, she gave a sigh of relief. She had completely forgotten to tell her husband what she had seen. It must have escaped her mind! All she wanted to do was to go home.

With his Latin background, he didn't help to soften the situation. "I could have killed you!" He yelled.

"That's enough of this nonsense! You will have to quit going to classes and blah! Bla! Bla! he went on.

She was too tired and filled with relief to worry about this outbreak. It was something she was used to. Tho'at other times this used to effect her very badly.

CHAPTER 29

MY CHILDREN

At first Pete seemed to have numerous problems at school. First of all he hated his new environment. Secondly his mother was studying so he couldn't go to her with all his problems. He missed all his friends and didn't seem to take much interest in anything. In a few words he found it hard to adjust. He grabbed every opportunity to protest, however silly it was. This proved that he couldn't handle the change.

But fortunately this was only temporary. A couple of months later he got into the swing of things and began to participate. His dynamic character soon drew many boys to him. He found this difficult to handle tho' because he preferred to choose his friends. He wasn't someone who liked to have many people around him.

Melani decided to pay a visit to the school, to meet all the teachers. The Director was very affable and assured her that parents were always welcome. But that she didn't have to worry too much about her children. All they need is time. Once they get into sports, there won't be a problem. Does Pete practise any? She mentioned that he was very good in soccer.

"That's what we are looking for, was he in the school team in Etobicoke?"

She nodded.

"Well, that's what he needs!"

That very week the councilor invited him to go to the soccer match that weekend. He happily agreed and was soon part of it and became one of the best players. It didn't take long before his marks in others subjects began to go up.

Kodi seemed to be a happy child. The moment she began with French, she was carried away by the teacher. Kodi could speak it fluently, so the teacher used this as an opportunity to make her take a higher course and gave her many magazines. Soon she became part and parcel of the school.

Pete began bringing boys home, at lunch time. There was always extra food.

"Let's go to Pete's house, we don't have to eat hamburghers!" They used to say. Most of them lived a little ways from the school. Melani was so happy with the change that she made sure that their friends were always very welcome.

Melani didn't quit University! She had a very strong will power which took her a long way and no doubt helped her cope with everything. Besides the atmosphere at home slowly began to change, for the better. They reached a happy medium, when everyone began to do their part. At last she thought, I can concentrate more on my studies. Not tha she didn't do her very best. It's just that it seemed as if she had more time. Sometimes she also got bot Kodi and Pete to give her a hand with some of her assignments. This filled them with great pride. The usually perfect mum, who knew everything was actually human and formed part of their lives.

Geo, used to accompany Pete to his soccer matches and sometimes the whole family went, too. On those occasions, they ended up going out for lunch together.

A couple of months later Kodi joined the school athlete team. At first she found the training a tad too hard. One day she came home bleeding, so we had to speak to the teacher to give her an opportunity to slow down a bit until she got physically fit. So instead of doing the same number of laps as the others, se did a little less than them until such time she could fit in with the group.

This school paid a great deal of attention on Sports. According to the Director, "Exercise, not only gets rid of the toxins of the body but it is also good for the soul. This school in Oakville, was one of the best in Ontario in sports and usually carried away most of the medals by the end of the school year. But the students also excelled in other subjects. Their students had no problems at the University. They had a very good, dynamic Science department which held competitions for creativity. Anyone who made a new invention received prizes. Usually at the end of the year besides the parents, the local companies were always invited, so that they could spot, the potential among the students.

All the Parents had the right to participate in school activities and had a say in it's development.

CHAPTER 30

THE PRIVILEGE

Kodi was requested to go to the Director's office. This usually happens if somebody had broken a very important school rule or to be given some negative news. This was the accepted opinion of the school.

Kodi was pretty nervous as she slowly walked towards his office.

She kept asking herself, "Is there anything I did wrong ….. No, as far as I am concerned I feel pretty comfortable with myself!"

She knocked and a pleasant voice said, "Come in!"

The moment she had entered the office, she discovered that Mr. Blondel was in a good mood. That made her relax. She now felt better.

"Kodi, before I go on, I should say that all your teachers are very pleased with you. I have received some glowing reports about your work, so that is one of the reasons why we decided to choose you, to give you an opportunity, which we hope you will be able to take advantage of. No doubt the final answer will not depend on us, though they rely on us a great deal, to find the suitable candidates.

"I am sure you must be wondering why you were called to the office and what I am talking about. Well, we received a very special offer from the Provincial Police Department and we thought it might interest you. No doubt our school is very honoured to have been requested and we would like to send the best students hoping they would qualify, for this great opportunity."

"There are some regulations they follow to qualify the students. According to their requirements, we feel that you could be a very suitable candidate. The Police Department of the Halton Board has introduced a new programme, well not exactly, it's the second year, specially directed toward the students. The first year had been successful and they would like to repeat it this year. The main idea being that students realise the importance of the work done by the Police. Together with the students they wish to work hand in hand to make the city a safe place for everyone to live.

Being Ethnic and Intelligent we thought you would make a great candidate. We emphasise on being Ethnic to show that Canada is a Multi-Racial community and that everyone should be treated equally, with equal rights and participate in the successful growth of this country. Since you come from a family of mixed cultures, with a knowledge of more than one language, and you are doing very well in your studies, we decided to talk to you about it. I emphasize that this doesn't guarantee your acceptation. But you never know unless you try.

This completely took the wind out of her sails. She was filled with mixed feelings. That day she walked around in a pensative mood. Yes, she had a lot of thinking, to do. At first she felt flattered to have been requested, but soon it was replaced with a scary feeling. The Police, what would that involve? I have never ever thought about joining the police, especially at this young age. I just completed fourteen. Maybe the Director is under the wrong impression about my age.

On arriving home she looked very subdued and serious.

"Try as I might I couldn't pry her mouth open to find out what was worrying her. It looked as if she was immersed in something terribly important. I decided to leave her alone. Eventually she is bound to come to me, in her own good time," Thought Melani. This she did, the very next day.

"Mum, I've filled in a form for a summer job. Now, this is no ordinary job! It's a special privilege and a very difficult one. I am not sure that I shall be accepted but I feel the possibility is great because I have been recommended, for it by Mr. Blundell, you know him, the Director of the school.

"Now what is it all about … or do you wish to talk about it? I knew you were pretty engrossed in something serious, but I didn't want to intervene because I felt that you needed some time, to yourself.

"Well it's going to be a kind of a learning experience with the Police force. They will be choosing only twelve students in the whole of Ontario. I just have to be patient and wait for their answer. Should they accept us we will be paid during the time we train and work. I am a bit nervous, but at the same time quite curious."

She sounded quite excited as she kept relating this to her mom.

"You never know. How long do you have to wait for an answer? Would you have an interview before?" Her mother kept plying her with questions. "As of this moment I know, no more." She said.

Doubtless to say she felt much better after having got this out of her system, as she was longing to tell someone about it.

The next day she went to the Councillor to tell him all about it. No doubt he wasn't in the dark. He then suggested, "Kodi, why don't you talk to the students who were chosen last here. They are here in the school." He then gave her a list of the names. Of course this is personal information, I am giving you because both the Mr. Blundell and I feel very strongly that you stand an excellent chance of being chosen."

She followed one of them and chose a discrete moment, when he was alone. "Daniel", she interrupted him as he was walking by. "May I talk to you for a moment?" "Sure", he answered very cordially. "What can I do for you?"

"I have just applied for this summer job, at the recommendation of Mr. Blundel, in the Police and I was wondering if you could tell me something about it. I am pretty curious about the whole thing and worried at the same time.!"

"Well, don't! First of all I feel sure you will be accepted. The job isn't easy but you will discover that it is extremely exciting. We literally do everything that the Police does with no exception. Knowing you as much as I do, you are going to enjoy it. I wish to see you there. After the experience, I am now, officially a cadet."

That day when she got home she told her mother about her experience about talking to the boy who was already in the Police force. "The students who were admitted last year thought the experience was well worth it. As a matter of fact most of them have actually joined the force. They are now cadets. This had been the original way of getting to mix with students and helping them to avoid internal problems within the schools.

Besides it was a way of getting in direct contact with eligible students, giving them the formation that's necessary to create an awareness of the problems, that occur in everyday life, no matter whether rich or poor, with no difference of colour or creed.

This was also a way to get closer to the hearts of the people. to find out how they really, think and feel. Dealing with the youth, with the tomorrow and to getting to know what makes our youth tick, what causes crimes at such early ages and to help create a favourable environment for young people to grow, thus making it a cleaner place, without drugs and where crime is nipped at the bud and not given room to grow.

"This idea has been innovative, ambitious and an expensive plan, implemented by The Chief of Police of the Hlaton Board, Mr. Maverick" said the Secretary.

Mr. Maverick said that he was prepared to sacrifice all he could towards crating a better society where people could live in peace and harmony and have high values.

A few days had hardly gone by when she was called for an interview. It was pretty informal as they had all the detailed information about her from the school. The officer who had interviewed her was very friendly and helped her relax. Most of the questions were all about her, her hobbies and her opinion of the police force.

Later she was given a psychological test. This wasn't very comfortable as they drive even, the sanest completely crazy. Since it was a computerised test, it was corrected instantly.

All this was done within the school premises so that the students wouldn't miss any classes. She was met by one of the co-ordinators and then directed to the school gymnasium. Later they were given a talk in the school gymnasium. They were briefed about what the job consisted of, and when they would have to incorporate explaining all that was required of them. The first couple of weeks they would be sent to the Cadet Training Centre and then they would be allotted a center and a cop with who, they had to work with. They did the very same job, just as a normal cop.

A tea-party was organised so that the whole group would get to know each other and meet their parents. Those who wished to bring any of their delicacies, were very welcome to do so. This would be one way of getting to know the different foods of different countries. Besides they would also get to meet the students who had, had this experience.

That afternoon Kodi was bubbling with energy she couldn't contain. She could hardly wait for her mother's arrival. Just that day Melani's lecturer was ill. So both Sharon and her were able to do their assignments earlier than usual, at the library and were able to go home, a couple of hours earlier than usual.

Seeing Kodi's face as she entered through the door she surmised that Kodi must have had some good news.

"Well, what's all the news? You look really excited, now out with it. I can hardly wait to hear it all.

"Mum here's the answer to my application!" She said as she handed over the letter to her mother, to be read.

This was a formal letter of acceptation given to each of the students, which had been signed by both the Police and the students. What surprised all the students was the compensation they would receive - $2000 This surely took the breath away when the students saw that. Quite a salary but of course no difference would be shown between the polic and them. They would be guided but had to act responsibly. They followed the same shifts, walked the streets, attended complaints, paid visits to families and also the prison. They had to be tained in the use of arms. Kodi was soon to learn that life in the Police was not all glamourous. They required strong and hardworking people.

The whole family congratulated her. Pete was a bit ruffled he wasn't chosen. Yes, he was a little disappointed. It didn't last long though, as his life was super active.

CHAPTER 31

THE INTRODUCTIONS

Kodi couldn't wait for the day of the party. This meant that she was officially admitted. She was up, earlier than usual and went for a short walk to curb her mounting excitement. That day seemed to come to a standstill. She couldn't help counting the time. The day dawned blue and beautiful. It was quite warm. She wore a long, sleeveless, beautiful pale green chiffon dress, which had a splash of red little flowers, to give it a cheerful, touch of summer. She had a scarf that matched the dress. This was going to be in Burlington, very near the water front. It not only gave her a touch of elegance but would come in handy. It could turn a bit cool in the evenings. She carried a pale red bag and matching sandals.

Giovani couldn't accompany them as he had been working in Toronto and would only return by 9 p.m. Melani accompanied Kodi. "I couldn't contain her excitement", she later told Gio. She kept pestering her mother to get ready.

"We are going to be late, as it is very far away."

"There could be a traffic jam!" Burlington was only 30 Kms from Oakville and the longest they could take was half an hour. But Kodi couldn't understand that there was ample time.

It was only 5:30 p.m.

So naturally they were the first to arrive and since nobody was there, they decided to go for a walk along the marine drive that was just a few yards from the Police Headquarters. This was an exhilarating walk. A very beautiful area where there numerous young people swishing past in their ski-doos, plying up and down and at times, some even daring to break speed-limits, although there were within reach of the Police. The lakeside was busy with numerous people who were sailing for pleasure while, still others were fishing. This made a very relaxing picture. There was a refreshing cool breeze blowing, so Kodi was happy to have carried her scarf.

Forty-five minutes later they decided to go back to the Quarters. Her credentials were checked and then all of them were given their uniforms. Each of them were given a couple of blue and white T-shirts, and a cap. They each had the emblem of the Halton Police.

One of the parents took charge and directed us to the kitchen where we could help lay out the food we had brought. Later introductions were made by those in charge and the parents got to meet others and soon everyone were busy exchanging anecdotes about their children. Other parents whose children had already been in the force had a lot of information to exchange, about their children's experiences. It didn't take long before everyone were busy cutting arranging and trying to find a dish or place to spread out their delicacies. The aroma tempted me to try out something but decided against it and waited until it was time for the party.

Kodi was soon part of her group. They were directed around. There were being given instructions about all that they had to do, in the forth-coming week. The young girls seemed to get carried away by the dashing officer who turned the heads of everyone, present. He was not only good-looking but had a very pleasant character. So the young boys and girls all took to him. He made them feel very comfortable and knew that they could count on him for anything that they needed. He was officially responsible for them. The following monday everyone of them had to incorporate.

Kodi was picked up around 7 a.m. They were taken to the head – quarters where each of them were given detailed instruction of all that they had to do and where they would have to operate from. The group was not going to be together. Each would be distributed among the different police stations in the Halton Region, where they were expected to follow the normal routine of those, that were in the force. Everyday they would follow the normal routes and also spent time working in the office which, to be frank, to most of the cops this was a great waste of time, just having to attend to long hours at courts or answering calls.

The general profile created by the often, ignorant public was that the police work just comprised of strutting around in their smart uniforms, arresting someone of and on and then letting them out through the back-door the very day or the next. Often than not, this could have been solved without their intervention. At other times there would be a valid reason but people would withdraw their complaint. This occurred when there was a problem within the family. Husband versus Wife could be the worst situations! One never knew how to re-act. Often than not it was a supposed – to- be mistake! This happened due the total dependence of the woman on the man. Sometimes it could be just the opposite, too.

Court cases were the same. They catch a criminal and the next day they are freed because they have great lawyers who always found a way around the law to get their clients free of all charges. Sometimes on bail at others there is a valid excuse for the offence and so on. So instead of peacefully trying to find a solution to problems, the problem becomes theirs, to solve. Hence a great deal of unnecessary bureaucracy.

One day the police decided to create an awareness among the citizens to help prevent petty crimes, like stealing from cars or even bigger ones like actually stealing cars. On the round they did that day, they discovered that 75% of the cars parked at the mall were left open and some of them had the keys inside. They left a note of warning inside. Fortunately they were always in twos, just in case someone felt like accusing them of breaking into their cars. One often came across one of these wise-cracks who lived, on pulling one of these. This was one way of instilling a respect for the police and to teach people how to participate in preventing crime, however insignificant, it may seem.

The growing number of terrorist actions could only be stopped, if everyone realised that they are duty bound to throw in their grain of sand in the prevention of such actions where people are being kidnapped, or threatened by organizations, often impossible to infiltrate without the help of the common man, the next door neighbour –

People know what is happening around us. There is always somebody watching. These people could save the lives of people, and save the government a great deal of money. What a wonderful world this would be if every citizen would realise the importance of working together and making our streets a safe haven.

Such actions like the shooting of babies in Scotland, the Oklahoma Bombing, The gas in the train in Japan, the 11th September and the 11TH March bombing could have been prevented, if people were more observant or realised that they could have prevented these acts if they had reported unusual happenings around them.

The most worrying experience and heart-breaking experience had been when Kodi had to participate in the search for one of the teenagers, who had been missing for a few days. This involved riding the police boat, just in case the body was thrown into the water and it would surface, at any time. This was one of the girls who usually went jogging around her area and was never found, inspite of the search which involved not only the police but special bodies and the public. All in vain.

The experience they received on a daily basis was very wide – a regular 8- hour working period which could be distributed in three shifts - morning, noon and night shifts. Kodi found it hard to adapt to the night shifts but adapt she did! The friendly Police officer who accompanied them were all exceptionally kind. They went out of their way to assure that their students were being prepared to face the realities of the daily life of any normal cop and softening it by grabbing a donut at breaks and having lunches together and helping them whenever necessary.

Life for Kodi had changed a great deal from being a student to a mature adult. She discovered that life wasn't very easy and that it was full of complications. It broke her heart to see so many young people go astray and get involved in drink and drugs due to their rough up-bringing. Ir-responsible parents who bring children into the world, without bothering about them, sometimes due to lack of time as they are too busy making money or trying to make a living. Broken families confuse children who do not know where to draw the line between right and wrong.

CHAPTER 32

HOLIDAY IN GENOVA

Melani's life seemed to become one hell of a run. She was living such a hectic life that one would have expected her to she neglect her family. No, she was able to swing it. Organization took control of her life and helped to run everything smoothly. At first she was running at break-neck speed but with the help of her family, who were true to their word she found that everything was within control. No doubt she had to burn the midnight candle. In her words, "this is the only quality time, when there was perfect silence and no one to disturb."

Fortunately she was able to grab her beauty sleep in the mornings. Naturally making do with less time than she had been used to. But she woke up fresh as a daisy. She discovered that she really didn't need more than five hours of sleep. The moment she touched bed she was dead to the world and so felt completely refreshed on waking up. At times Gio felt a wee bit neglected as Melani divided more of her time between her studies and her children. So to compensate she made sure that during the weekends they did something very special together.

Melani was determined to prove to her children her worth and to give them a sense of responsibility. They were proud of her. But examination times were the worst they were nerve -racking as a display of flying tempers often became the norm of the day and at times it surely did upset someone's applecart. This was when she would cook special foods or bring them little surprises to help the kids relax and at the same time keep Gio calm.

The year flew by and soon it was holiday time. The kids did well in school and so did Melani. So the family tried to spend as much time together, to make up for the tight schedule they all had to follow. This was when Gio took the family by surprise. "Why don't we go to Genoa, next month. It's high time all of you got to meet your grandparents. The company has been doing well, so we were given a bonus. That's why, I decided to spend it exclusively on our holiday. Here are the tickets!

Both Kodi and Pete were really excited. Kodi hugged her father who she adored. While Pete was all plans about what he was going to do. In a moment he brought out the map and the encylopedia. Together they went through the pages, one with the map the other with the encylopedia.

"I am sure you are going to enjoy living at the sea -side. Pete maybe you could go fishing with your grandfather. All the family seemed to be very excited and they are all looking forward to meeting you."

Turning toward his wife he said, "You don't sound as if you are pleased!" he asked, looking at her face completely, lost in thought.

She was brought back to earth from her reverie. "Oh no, I guess this is a great surprise! It's just that all this all is so sudden. You didn't discuss this with me. But all the same this is a wonderful gift for the family!"

She didn't sound too convinced. Gio disregarded it, thinking that this was just a temporary feeling because he hadn't asked for her opinion earlier.

Little did he realise the heinousness of the situation! She had too many things in her mind.

First of all, she was going to meet the family she had hardly heard about and never seen.

"Why would he suddenly decide to do so, right now?"

"Was life playing her a dirty trick?" After all these years why would he choose this year – the year she had come in contact with someone, who she had tried to oust from her memory?

Mario! He was back to haunt her. She got so involved with her studies that she had little time to think about him. No doubt she thought she had done that successfully - "Intelligent", she thought, at that time. This couldn't be happening to her. All her feelings seem to come back, now, all the more - stronger than ever!

She recalled his words, "I am sure we are going to meet again. This is not going to be our last goodbye!"

"Since Kodi will be working until the fifteenth of August, I decided to take my vacations from then, on. Pete you could also find a job till such time, so that you will have some extra money to spend. We could leave on Saturday, sixteenth. What do you think about it?" He turned to Melani, who readily agreed, without knowing what they had been talking about, when she realised that everyone had turned to hear whether she had anything to say.

Melani lay awake for hours that night, although she pretended to fall asleep the moment she got into bed.

She kissed Gio, "I think you were very thoughtful to have planned this holiday for us. Do you think we will be fine there. I don't know your parents and I am looking forward to meeting them. It's a pity we have waited such a long time. Thanks once again, I am sure we are all going to enjoy it. We have had a lot of excitement for today and I am very tired, so I'm going to sleep, goodnight."

"Before you go to sleep I must tell you, the reason for my decision. I have been worried about my parents for some time. They are getting on, in age and I know that my mother hadn't been keeping very well recently, at least that was what my brother told me."

She lay awake, way into the night as Giovani kept snoring. Thoughts of the past came flooding back to her as she recalled the day she met Mario. Yes, she had received one letter from him, which she decided to ignore. Fortunately it didn't fall into Gio's hands. He seldom opened the letter-box, so she was lucky. She had even torn his card. "that's the end of it – one way of eradicating him from her brain - so out of her head he was supposed to be as she had decided, which she thought she had, until Gio dropped this bomb-shell. Keeping busy, was the best thing she could have done, but this!

"Why oh! Why should this thing happen to me?" she kept asking herself. She thought that she had successfully blocked away those treasured moments she maintained until she began her classes at the university. But now! It all came rushing back!"

No one in the family guessed what had happened inside her.

More than a year had passed since he had left an indelible mark on her life. Her body trembled with excitement as she once again went through each of those moments, in Virgina ..... just a few hours together. It seems impossible but life plays dangerous tricks with the lives of innocent people sometimes, creating situations that are incomprehensible. She was now excited but at the same time terrified of getting to see him again. This wouldn't be the same turf! It would be his turf and what a turf –my in-laws! What a contradictory situation.

She then brushed all these thoughts aside when her intelligence took over.

"Don't worry, he must be married by now! He's too handsome not to have been captured by some woman or other" With that she decided to put him out of her head and continue with her routine.

They decided to leave on the 16th. Of august. A week before their departure, both the children wanted to do a lot of shopping for clothes.

"If I were you I'd save that money for Genoa, where you could get the best of clothers – rather the most fashionable and of a higher quality and a better price.

"No dad, one of my friends told me how very expensive Italy was. Anyways, we can't go empty-handed. So both Kodi and I decided to but collective gifts. just a few!"

On the day of their departure, neither Kodi nor Pete wanted to have any breakfast.

"You better have something as you never know what happens in airports. Most often there are delays. So she convinced them to have their orange –juice and a couple of slices of toast.

At 11 a.m. Gio called for a cab and together they packed all the things into the boot, of the cab!

Once at the airport, everything seemed to go smoothly until they went through security. As Pete passed through the alarm went off.

This not only shook the customs' officers but the rest of us. They emptied his pockets, but found nothing. Not until he was asked to take off his clothes did they realise that he had his keys around his neck. Everyone broke into a hearty good laughter, after this sudden scare. Especially these days after so many bomb scares, most of the autorities are pretty sensitive about the least suspicious actions.

CHAPTER 33

THE DEPARTURE

ir Canada flight number 434 will be boarding, in a few minutes, at gate number 14. Giovani turned to look for the kids and they weren't to be seen anywhere around.

"Giovani, why don't you check the washrooms. I'll take care of the luggage."

After having walked up and down, it suddenly dawned on him… he knew where to find them! Pete seemed to be pretty engrossed in something while his sister was browsing around, in the duty-free shops. He gave Pete a slight tap which startled him.

"Come on, it's time to leave. We are boarding now, unless you wish to stay here! Now where's your sister" he asked. Just at that moment hearing her father's voice she came toward them.

"With the great reluctance on their part, he managed to drag them from there. They were carried away by the numerous things, they saw there. But now they had no alternative but to follow their dad.

On board both wanted the window seats, so here began another argument. So we decided that both would take turns. Kodi very quickly said, "Let Pete be first!"

"Oh! that's very sweet of you," said Melani.

Little did she realise that Kodi wanted to have the view when she was half way toward Genoa. She had travelled before and had seen the departure route many times. This seemed to solve the present problem and everyone were happy

Gio seemed a bit nervous and usually found an excuse to complain if we were alone. But now with the kids around he just held his breath. Melani suspected that he was afraid of planes. But he completely disagreed saying, "It's just the waiting at airports that completely puts me off. In a way that was a bit irritating for anyone who just sat put, doing nothing. No doubt at times this could drag on, due to bad weather conditions at winter time. Many airports weren't prepared for take-offs and landing when there was fog.

Pete enjoyed observing how the plane got ready for take-off as he watched the revving of engines, when it slowly but steadily began to rise, how the wheels folded inwards as it kept climbing higher. Looking downwards, the sky line of Toronto could be seen with the numerous lights that kept blinking in all directions as they reflected each other, on this windy afternoon.

"Kindly keep your seatbelts on until you are advised! We request you now to pay attention to all the instructions on security measures. Most people ignored this which could be very foolish. Newspapers and magazines were distributed. Kodi and Pete decided to play a game of chess.

The cheerful voice of the Captain was heard on the speaker, half an hour later. "We are flying at a height of 5000ft and we shall be flying over the Hudson bay... he gave some other information but suddenly his voice broke ……. Under your seats you will find your safety jackets. Kindly take them out and follow instructions which will not only be flashed on the screen but demonstrated by the airhostesses. This is only a security measure, I repeat. The plane then took a sudden dip, that made most people who… ah… ah.

Once more another announcement, "Due to a minor problem we shall be returning to the airport. This is a special announcement, please follow the instructions of the airhostesses without giving them any problems. They will be going around. I repeat that this is a minor problem, so relax and follow the screen." His voice sounded very calm, so it really didn't frighten the passengers.

One of them distributed candy, to help calm the people. Fright reflected on some of their faces.

They had travelled umpteen times but this had never ever happened before, so they realised there must have been a serious problem. Both Kodi and Pete looked at their parents' faces for reassurance. Finding them calm, they relaxed. Little did they realise how terrorised both Melani and Gio were, but they dared not show it to their children. They had travelled a great deal, but this had never ever happened before, so they realised there must have been a serious problem.

Turning to them, they said, "Pay great attention to all the instructions,!" Then checking to see if they had found the safety jackets and before they showed them how to use it, they had already had them on. They must have thought that this was one of those fake practises, they had to do in schools to make sure, that students knew how to re-act in emergencies.

"All passengers are requested to stay in their seats. Now don't panic this is just a security measure! Will all the passengers please remove their shoes and follow the airhostess' instructions. Look for the exit doors nearest to you, but don't move, now! We would like those people with babies and very old people to exit first, on arrival. Now this will only be done on arrival at the airport. Keep your seatbelts on, we repeat and please don't try to get out of your seats until further notice."

They had everything under control tho' fear reflected on nearly all the faces, but fortunately none broke into hysteria. All of them prepared themselves, for the worst. But seeing nothing really unusual but the constant dips and climbs, one experiences when an aircraft gets into an airpocket; most passengers kept calm.

The calm voice of the Captain came on the air again, "In a few minutes we will be landing. Just as we are landing and about to touch ground the security doors will fly open and chutes would be let down. Everything is under control, we just don't want anyone to panic. If you follow the instructions you will be out of the plane before you know it. Thank You!" Gio and some others went to give a hand, with the disabled and babies. Now it was clearly seen that some people were getting agitated.

Suddenly Kodi began to scream before her mother managed to choke it, "Look mum, the wings on fire! "She was trembling as she said it and so was I.

Fortunately it didn't take long before a bump. bump…bump of the aircraft as it crashed landed.

Yes, the whole airport was covered with flashing lights from fire-fighters, ambulances, buses and police cars with their sirens full blast.

It seemed as if all the firemen in town had arrived, all at the same time. This would make anyone's hair stand, just watching. But there seemed to be a deadly calm as the passengers prepared themselves for disembarkation, through the chute, no doubt. The kindness and patience of the stewards and hostesses, and some of the passengers, helped solve some minor problems.

You could imagine the plight of the terrified passengers, but yet, some of them still had the courage to applaud the Pilot as he finally touched ground, knowing that everything was going to be well.

Just at that moment the ice was broken, when an old lady was suddenly woken up, from a supposed –to-be deep slumber.

"Oh, have we arrived? "She asked.

"Yes the revving of the engines usually put me to sleep, everytime, I fly.

A couple of the passengers who still had a sense of humour, couldn't control their laughter, which had a calming effect on the rest of the passengers, in such a tense situation. With hearts in our mouths, we all waited for our turn to come, to go down the chute. The chutes were down in a fleeting second and there were many people ready to help. Some passengers scared and claustrophobic had to be pushed down the chute when they began to protest. The speed and efficiency of the hostesses and the ground staff, convinced all the passengers of their safety. Yes, everyone landed safe and sound, without even a scratch.

The Pilot, doubtless to say was fantastic and knew his job!

In no time, the firemen were busy putting off the fire.

No sooner than everyone had been evacuated from the aircraft, an announcement was heard.

"All passengers are requested to use the Executive Lounge, where they could relax and where their individual needs would be attended to. Lunch will be followed. On the whole there was great order. Every passenger was attended to, personally, as professionals took complete control of the situation. Free telephone calls could be made to family members or whoever you need to contact.

In the meantime we will be transferring all your personal belongings to another aircraft. Should any of you wish to make any changes feel free to approach the attendants or the ground staff. They will give you all the necessary advice, you need.

A few of the passengers who were relaxed, approached the counter to pick up their food coupons. Maybe after a meal, we shall be able to clarify our thoughts. In the meantime others crowded around the front desk until order was restored.

"Will our cases and all our personal belongings be taken care of?"

"I am sorry, but I would like to return home, could you help me?"

"Yes, we'll give a refund or if necessary we could postpone your trip fo another day."

"No, although the aircraft is being taken care of, you will not be flying in the same one. I add, that there was no serious damage, to the aircraft. A bird had got into the ellis and that's what caused the damage. So while your cases are being loaded to another aircraft and other necessary changes, to be made, you have enough time to have a meal and relax in the lounge. Once again we beg you to forgive us for the inconveniences caused. Should you require anything that's within our power you can count on it."

The cafeteria was filled with the clattering of plates, forks and spoons. The waiters were rushing around to please such an unexpected influx of people, many of them just giving way to their controlled anxiety, so their voices were a tad, too loud for such a group of generally subdued group of people. Others were at the bar, sipping their drinks trying to get back their sanity.

"Don't worry Sally, we could return home if you like. I know you did this trip just to please me. I still have time, so, should you decide to go later, after we have got over this shock, we could do it. I won't be disappointed, in any way," said Mr. Jameson to his wife, when he realised that she was completely shaken up.

Still another passenger, Don tried to convince his 70-year old wife to cancel the trip because he was worried that she wouldn't be able to handle any more excitement for the day. I guess all the planning has been a lot more interesting than this disaster. I'd rather we stayed put and avoid the hazzle of going from one country to another. Instead why can we keep to our original plan of renting a caravan and travelling around our own province?" He ended when she said not a word. This was the lady who had slept through all the confusion and was the most relaxed passenger.

"Oh, no dear. I feel perfectly well! This has only been a minor inconvenience. Things worse than this could happen to us just sitting at home. Do you remember Mrs. Hamsted? She got killed by a car that lost control and landed in her patio while she was doing her gardening. Please Don, let's not change our plans, I've been looking forward to this trip for a very long time."

Don was satisfied that his wife was fine and yes, they decided to continue on the trip.

Yet another, swore that she would never ever board another aircraft in his life. "I've always been terrified of flying, but my wife convinced me to come on this trip.

"Arthur", she said two weeks ago, "I've just bought us two tickets to go on a trip to Italy!"

He was so taken aback and asked, "Where did you get the money, we have so many problems. Why, the hell did you go and spend the little money we have?" He angrily shouted.

"I won the lottery, she said smiling. I got $20,000 so I decided to do something we would never dream of normally doing.

Do you remember saying one day, "I have never visited my mother's hometown, I would like to do so one day as she used to tell us how beautiful Genoa was. I made this promise to myself ten years ago, that one day I would take you there. So since then every week I played the Lotto. So here you are! We'll be fine, let's go!" She had just won the lottery and could never have dreamed of doing something like this before.

"Well, why not? "He excitedly agreed and he was happy he did!

While they were having a meal Gio asked his children, "Do you still wish to go on this trip?"

Unanimously they added without a doubt, "No way!"

"I am not going to lose out, on telling my friends about all that had happened. Won't they laugh at me, if I tell them that I chickened out, at the last minute." Pete boldly spoke out.

"Neither am I going to miss these vacations. Didn't I work extremely hard? I am also looking forward to meeting the family and getting to know a new country - a new city – a different culture, especially having to visit a seaside town. Mom, what about you? Don't you have anything to say?" She passed the ball onto the other court.

"Gio, you're not serious, after all this planning! Yes, I agree with the children we are going!" That's the end of the story.

Three hours later, everyone, with the exception of the few people who decided not to travel that day, were on the aircraft, once again.

The moment they got on board, Melani said, "Let's say a prayer of thanks and ask God to take us safely to and back home. "They joined their hands together and closed their eyes.

"God has given us another opportunity to live. Gio, do you recall that car accident, ten years ago. Well, we escaped by the skin of our teeth, without a single scratch on either of us, nor with the car. We were driving down a mountainous slope on a very rainy day. It was a cold, dark summer's day. At first it just seemed like a thunder storm. We continued on our way hoping that it would soon stop. Instead of abating, it turned into a torrential rain. The roads were completely flooded. It took complete control of the car and just dragged the car to the edge of a precipice.

I still think it was a Miracle.

"Our car got stuck on just one wheel in the mud. You kids were just three and four, but neither of you screamed, which may have helped to act calmly. I then got out, opened your doors and slowly took you out one by one and then papa got out, the last. The car swayed a bit, but stayed. The drivers who came to our aid thought it was something incredible. We did this all very quickly but slowly. The slightest false movement would have taken us down to 40mts. below."

"I just can't forget that nightmarish experience!" added Gio.

"I was on the point of jumping out, in a split second at first. It was a logical, fight for survival.

But I withheld. Maybe that could have been why the car wouldn't move as I was the heaviest of the family. After all of you were out. I jumped out very fast.

At that moment I thought that my life was about to end.

But no, we're here, together again in one piece after experiencing something more. You would have a lot to tell your children when you have your own!" ended Gio with a sigh.

Moments later a couple of guys came to our aid. With their aid, with great difficulty, we managed to put the car back onto it's four wheels. We were dumb-founded but couldn't evade looking over the precipice, inspite of the heavy rain. To top it all, nothing had happened to the car, we drove on, as if nothing had happened to us. I guess it all happened within a long one-minute period!

ARRIVAL IN GENOVA

Melani managed to get the children all spruced up in their Sunday best.

Well, she really didn't have to do much as they could very well take care of themselves, half an hour before landing.

Geo looked his, cool, calm self, which I doubt he felt. I saw that sad look back on his face again. I wanted to ask him about it, but with the children around it was impossible. I had completely forgotten all about it, as he was a wonderful husband and father.

"It has been a long time since I have visited my parents. This is going to be a family re-union. I am sure we are all going to have a wonderful time. "Turning towards to the children," he said, "Your grandfather has great plans for you, but he didn't give me a hint about it. I hope you have something for them. Naturally bought with your own savings.!" He teased.

Melani was a wee bit nervous as she had only met one of the brothers and didn't know the sisters. His brother Pietro had married an Italian girl from his home town. Since then he had gone back to help his parents with their business. He had two children Toni and Lisa. They were twins and three years younger than Kodi.

Yes, it's going to nice for the children to meet the rest of the family. So far it had kind of being one-sided. Gio never seemed interested in going home, except for flying visits when either his father or mother was ill, most often not lasting more than a few days. Although his sisters didn't live in the same house, I was told they were walking distance from the house.

"I can see the sea," shouted Kodi, who had managed to reclaim her place, at the window seat.

"Papa, would we have a boat? Do you think we could go sailing around this beautiful area?" joined in Pete

"I can actually see through the blue, crystal, clear water.

This could be seen as the aircraft took a dip and began flying pretty low, until it turned towards the airport, getting ready for landing.

"I was filled with mixed feelings.

A great curiosity to meet the family grew inside me and at the same time I was a bit worried wondering how they would accept me. Yes, I had met his parents, at the wedding. They seemed to be very nice people. It had been too short a period of time. We really didn't get to speak very much to each other. Besides I couldn't speak the language either. They were in a great hurry to get back to Genoa, as they couldn't be away from the farm and the fishing industry they were involved in.

According to Geo life there had changed a great deal for the better. His family had become successful. Yes, Gio had kept to his word. He had faithfully sent his parents money.

And we were, and none-the less so was I rather excited. As the aircraft was about to touch the tamac, I felt the butterflies playing havoc in my stomach.

"Is something worrying you? You look rather pale!" asked Gio when he saw her shiver. He mistook it for her nervousness due to the harshness of the rough landing as the plane came to a shuddering stop, which did terrify the already tense passengers. They finally breathed a sigh of relief. "I think we have had enough for one day!" said one of them. Everyone seemed to begin chattering all at once as the passengers were all up grateful to have landed in on piece.

Neither of the two could be kept in their seats the moment the seat-belt signs were off. plane came to a shuddering stop which made the passengers hold on tight to their seat. "I think we have had enough for one day," said one of them holding tight to her seat, as most of the passengers breathed a sigh of relief

With his knapsack on his shoulders Pete, he impatiently waited for his turn and was the first to walk out of the aircraft and down the stairs.

Young, dashing and spritely he walked into the airport drawing welcome smiles from everyone guiding the people along the way.

On arriving at the airport we had to go through customs as usual. This was long-drawn – a bit on the disorganised line. It took us 45 minutes to go through. Once at the carousel we waited for the baggage. This seem to drive us completely crazy, especially the children. It took a long time and when it came through, we were very fortunate to get all of ours. But many people seemed terribly irritated as all their bags hadn't come through.

We could hear the attendants at the information desk patiently, saying, "We regret this had happened. It was due to that minor accident. If you fill in this form giving us details of colour, size and brand name of the case and your address we will contact you as soon as we find it. As a compensation you could buy the clothes you need and we will reimburse you 50% of the expense. Should you wish to spend the day here and wait, we shall put you up in a hotel. We feel sure that your luggage would be in, on the next flight. But you don't have to wait here. We will take it, to you wherever you are, going to be."

Some were very upset as they were on a tour.

Armed with the telephone number of the airport and a code to trace the information, grumbling some left. Others decided to wait for the next flight, which was expected in four hours.

They had hardly passed through the gate when, "Mi Bambino come sta? Accoglienza a Genova" his grandmother hugged Pete, as he looked identical to his father. Surprised he hugged back.

"Mama!" Gio had his arms round his mother. Soon there were hugs and kisses from all directions. Gio had made sure that his children, had seen the photographs of everyone, before they went on this trip.

Gio suddenly remembered Melani, who kept a low profile and waited in the background until it was her turn.

"You must forgive our impoliteness, in all this excitement we nearly forgot you. Thank you for coming. This is such a privilege to have all the family together. We are going to make sure that you have a very relaxing holiday here. We are proud of all the work that you do. How do you do all that?"

"Without the support of the family it would have been nearly impossible to do it!" she said. Soon she was introduced to the others who she hadn't met.

There were two limousines waiting outside. Kodi nudged her brother, "Eh aren't we V.I.P's!" said Kodi.

"Of course you are!" interrupted their uncle Tino. "Now come with me! Melani, you could also join us as there's more space in here!" Just before they started Gio shouted, "You're in good hands! Tino could point the interesting sites en route. The trip is going to take about an hour. If you are not comfortable, I could join you there. With that he left. Tino resulted to be the perfect host. The trip was most enjoyable, with Tino throwing in his sense of humour.

The car stopped in front of a very impressive house. Gio's father was at the door hopping around with his crutches. "He had fallen down the stairs just a week ago and has it have it in plaster for about a month, but he is in no pain whatsoever." Explained Tino.

"How are you Melani, after the long trip – which to me has been unusually long. Fortunately Gio called and told us that you were going to be delayed by a few hours. You look tired so you better have something cold to drink, it would refresh you. "At that moment, a lady came with a tray with fresh lemon juice for everyone. It was iced, so very apt for a sunny afternoon, in summer.

Then he turned to his grandchildren. At first they were a wee bit shy, but a fleeting second later they both ad their arms around him giving him, a hug. You could see he was clearly excited to see them. They weren't used to all the kissing and the hugging but a look from the mother reminded them of all the instructions she had given them before their departure. "Don't forget the Italians are very affectionate and demonstrative! So you follow them." It didn't take them long to adjust to their surroundings. I could see that their grandmother could hardly take her eyes off them.

Suddenly Melani couldn't take it all, she needed to be quiet for a few moments. The tone of their voices needed adjusting to, as all Latin people speak a tone, too loud, more so when they are excited and then so many people, together. She felt her head spin a we bit. So the moment they were shown to their rooms, she lay down for a bit.

Kodi and Pete were very excited with everything around them. Beteen Tino and their cousins they were soon shown around. A few moments later they dashed into the room," Mom, can we have a swim, right now? "They both asked filled with excitement.

"Of course you may, now you are on holiday., in the sense I would like you to be very thoughtful of the others and then enjoy all you can. Make sure that you respect everyone and follow their rules. Yes, but do tell me all that is happening around you and if you have to leave the house with anyone. Also find out what time is dinner-time. After you have a swim make sure you have a shower. I shall be down in an hour's time.

They were off, in the twinkling of an eye after they got into their swimsuits.

Melani had a respite. She had some time, to herself. Gino hadn't come up with, as it was normal he had so much to talk about.

"This was just like the moments when I visited my mother and all the sisters start chinwagging for hours on end "

So she was happy to be alone for a few moments. Unbeknownst to herself, she fell into a deep sleep. When she woke up she realised that her slumber had taken a good one hour. She felt terribly embarrassed, had a quick shower, donned a pale blue dress, checked the mirror to sees whether she was presentable. Satisfied with herself, she walked down the stairs. The sleep had refreshed her greatly. and she really looked looked very beautiful. A whistle from her brother-in –law, told her so.

Turning to his brother, he said, "You better be careful of your wife, we the Italians, as you know are very open-minded and know how to admire pretty women, so don't let her out of your sight, my dear brother!"he teased.

Marian, the mother laughed and said, "He's very naughty, but he's right. Gio has good taste!"

Soon the family got together. Everyone seemed very interested in talking to her. Both his sister and his sister-in –law were very friendly. The ambiance was so friendly that she felt as if she formed an integral part of the family. This got rid of her doubts and decided she was going to make the most of it.

"What would you like to drink?" asked Marian

"A shandy would be fine. "Gino made one for her and they went to the terrace which overlooked the sea. To her this was just a beautiful picture postcard. They sat facing the sea while they had some pistachio, olives and pastiani.

Each one wanted to grab her attention. They had so much to talk about. Gino's father brought out some photographs of Gino when he was a child. One of them was really comical where both the brothers were having a fight in the sea-shore. Tino said, "I think Gino suddenly fell, hitting me accidentally. Suddenly a big wave came dashing onto the shore dragging the two of us. a few moments later, I managed to get on my two feet and for a moment I was terrified when I couldn't see Gino. Then I turned to my left I could see him fighting the waves to come back to shore, so I swam after him. I didn't have to go far when another washed the two of us back to shore." It was a bit dangerous as the tide was changing. Fortunately we realised that we had enough time to run back to the shore. We were told that the tide changes every six hours. The beach we were at isn't the safest beach because at high tide, the beach completely disappears.

The picture was taken at the right time to show how terrified they both looked. Each one spoke a bit about their families and about things that happened there in the last few years. Soon it was dinner time.

The dining room was quite spacious. It had 14 straight backed -chairs with beautiful tapestry with the scene of a couple lying under a tree and a couple of children beside them.

The carpets were of pure wool. But something about it was distinctly different from many of the carpets she had ever seen. " Aren't these carpets really beautiful?

Gio's father went on to explain how he had come by it.

"That carpet was bought in Turkey while I was on a trip. One of my friends was Turkish. He took me to a shop in Istanbul, where he said they had the best carpets of he country. "

He continued, "It was quite a ceremony to buy one, unless you didn't care about the quality. The design, the colour and it's depth and the quality of the dye is very important. It is more a friendly exchange instead of a bargain, having to be very patient and ready to listen to the salesman who seem to love each piece and takes the time to bring out the beauty of the carpet and the importance of each piece. No doubt we were served tea which was part of the ceremony. Smoking the hookah was done among friends. Fortunately I could excuse myself when I said that I suffer from asthma and my friend supported me!" It was indeed an interesting experience. The curtains matched the colouring of the walls which was of a pastel salmon of very fine linen. The blinds were of a darker shade in velvet. One look around was enough to show you that they were a very well-to -do family.

The dinner was soon served. It was more a light supper because they realised that all of us were very tired after the long delay, at the airport. Pete was responsible for the delicious pizzas that were served. It hadn't taken him long, to get friendly with both the grandparents and when asked what he wanted for supper he immediately asked for pizza. "This is not going to be an imitation, but the real thing! Isn't it grandma?" This was followed by the specialty of the family which was (DESERT TYPICAL OF ITALY)

Both the children took turns between mouthfuls to explain all that they had gone through, not giving Gio a chance to explain. Surprisingly Kodi intervened to give detailed explanation of her part of the play - - how she had seen the wing on fire. Both the parents gave a deep sigh of relief to know that after all was said and done, it only turned out to be more of a fright than anything.

"Dad," asked Kodi, "Didn't you enjoy going down the chute?"

"Not exactly! I was hoping and praying that we were all, out of it before the aircraft caught on fire and we were trapped. Tension was the word, to describe the situation, mildly. "Everyone's faces were punctuated between awe and great relief.

"You were very fortunate that you not only had a fantastic pilot, who was very professional but had the presence of mind and the capacity to have been able to avoid, a deadly crash and to have acted on time. He really deserves a medal." said Toni

"So, that's why you were delayed so much!" said his mother.

Gio didn't want to explain all that had been happening when he called them from the airport in Toronto as he didn't want to unnecessarily, worry either his parents nor the rest of the family.

"We were a bit worried at first but then, since you didn't say why you were delayed we mistakenly thought that, it could have been a normal summer delay, due to the influx of passengers and the numerous flights that take off from all these big airports. It's generally a vicious chain, if one flight is delayed, others follow unless it's a night flight when pilots usually make up for lost time, without major problems.

By the time dinner was over everyone was ready for bed with the exception of Gio. Melani was happy to go to bed. It had been a couple of nights since she had slept well. She brushed her teeth, changed into her nightee and was off to bed listening to the lullaby of the sea as she kept one of the windows open.

CHAPTER 35

THE NEXT DAY

A complete silence reigned over the house, when Melani woke up. Gio was snoring next to her as usual. It was pretty clear that he must have had drunk a lot the previous night. The family must have had a lot to talk about. "Strange, I didn't even hear him come. I usually wake up at the slightest noise. I guess the day had taken it's toll on me. I feel as if I had slept for a good 8- hours."

This helped her to overcome the jetlag. She just loved the first hours of the day. Once she was ready, making sure not to disturb Gio, she tip-toed to the toilet, had a wash and wore a cool, white dress. She put up her hair and looked for the hat she had brought. Carrying a pair of sandals in her hand, not wanting to disturb anyone, as not a sound was heard, she walked quietly down the stairs. She had to walk around a bit, to finally find a way out.

The day, dawned bright and beautiful. She stopped to look through one of the bay –windows and was held spell-bound. The view was breath-taking!

"I must get a closer view of it! "She said to herself.

No sooner had she opened the door, when, she was startled.

"Borjourni Melani! Did you sleep well?"

"Yes, I found the bed so comfortable, with the satin sheets that it didn't take me long to fall asleep."

"Did you like your room? Come along this way! You can join us for breakfast in the terrace!"

It was Mr. Fellini. He must have observed her trying to find a door, but didn't want to shout out to her from the terrace, lest he would disturb those who were sleeping.

"I am very surprised you have woken up so early. People generally take a couple of days to overcome the difference of hours. It usually happens to me, everytime I travel and have to adjust to the change of hours. Your face doesn't show the ravages of the jetlag nor all the tension you have been through! "

"Well, I am just one of those very fortunate people who could make do with just a few hours of deep sleep. The University had trained me for that. If not it would have been impossible for me to handle all that I had to do. "

The house overlooked some rugged cliffs on one side and as you leaned against the railings, you could the waves lash against the rocks sending up a spray of foam, that actually kissed her face. She was so thrilled that she couldn't hide the exhilaration she felt within. The house commanded a view of the most picturesque surrounding coast-line.

"There at the bottom, you can see our boat." Pointed Fellini.

She was dumb-founded. Her husband had never mentioned that his parents had lived so well.

"That looks a gorgeous yacht! "she exclaimed with surprise in her voice. Expensive –no doubt about it! She thought to herself. She soon discovered that Fellini was not a presumptuous man.

"How can one go down to the boat? I can't see a way down. It looks impossible to get there!"She asked with a curiosity on her face.

"Oh, yes! All you have to do is dive down from here. It's an easy drop. You can't miss it. Besides you would not get hurt as the whole boat is lined with silk and foam, so no one could get hurt!" Appeared Tino as he said that.

"I asked, why didn't you brush off some of that sense of humour you have in you, to your serious brother!" As everyone joined in laughter..

"Well I don't know if Gino told you that, that wouldn't be a big problem for me, as I won the diving championship in High School!"

It was now his turn to change from a look of admiration mixed with surprise, at me.

"Of course, there's no doubt about you", joined Gino as he entered the terrace. How did I forget to tell you about it!" Keeping a straight face.

"That calls for a glass of champagne!" As everyone applauded. Melani together with Gino burst into laughter. and she said, "I got you, didn't I? We're even now!"

"Now, let's get serious. "No more teasing," as Gino added, "I am very hungry. Let's have breakfast

Before they adjoined to the dining room, "Come this way," said Mr. Felini as he guided her around the house. She then saw a white ornamental gate. which continued on to be a railing but from where they were it wasn't easily distinguishable. He opened it and then pointed to a flight of stone steps, maybe about a hundred, that led down to the quayside. On either side there was a wall which had flowers falling down it's sides. She couldn't contain her excitement. "How beautiful this is. I had no idea what a fantastic place you had here.

She loved the sea and so did her children. Strange as it may seem Gio preferred the mountains. The kindly man seemed to have taken to her.

"Yes, I can see you are anxious to go down. We shall do that as soon as we have had breakfast. Let's not keeping the others waiting. They should all be up now."

"It's surprising that Gio had woken up so early after having gone to bed so late. I guess he doesn't want to miss anything and he must have slept well."

He told his wife later. "Melani seems to have the heart of a child, she enjoys nature so much and seem to get carried away by it."

While they were walking towards the house Mr Fellini asked her, "Why have you taken so long to come here to visit us. I wrote askng Gio to bring you and the family here, but I guess he is a very busy person."

She was taken by surprise and not knowing what to say, she agreed with him, adding, "He works too much –a workaholic, no doubt."

He continued in a sad tone, we hardly receive any news from you either. The only way to know something about you is through his brother, Tino. He generally keeps us informed about everything that is happening. Not that Gio is very communicative! "With that he let out a deep sigh. She turned to look at him, gave his hand a reassuring squeeze, when she saw sadness written all over his face and for a moment he looked a pathetic, worn −out figure and my heart went out to him − this man who seemed gentleness itself.

Why does Gino do this to him. She realised that something was worrying him. It clearly reflected on his face, quite a similar lost, sad look that she had sometimes seen on her husband's face. I guess, in this way he wants to block away the past. He must have told you all about it."

This time I am going to make sure you have such an unforgettable holiday that, this will not be the first and the last trip you make here, but many, many more. You have no idea how happy you have made the whole family, especially my wife and I.

She reassured him that from then on he was going to get all the news about them. "I promise to keep in contact I am not a very good at letter −writing. But you will be a great priority, for me!"

"She was tempted to pursue the subject but held back as she intuitively felt that she may tread on dangerous ground and decided to drop it, which she didn't have to do.

"There you are! Do you like the place?" asked Mama Felini as everyone called out to her. "You have a gorgeous place!" exclaimed Melani.

"Aren't you hungry. I am famished," said Pete as he and Kodi appeared, from nowhere.

She decided to brush off the negative thoughts that began to creep in, "No", she told herself. "There's no time for fear or worry. It was time to enjoy every moment. This is a great break for me. I can't ask for anything more. I didn't have the remotest idea that this place had existed. I wonder why Gio, preferred to ignore it all. besides the stories he had told me didn't tell me that he belonged to such a well-to-do family, who live in this exclusive area.

"Why? Why? This was a million dollar question she kept asking herself. She wondered if she'd get an answer. The family seemed to be very friendly and warm. Even the sister who at first she thought wasn't friendly, she was soon to learn that it was just shyness on her part. Her children were equally friendly tho' didn't take well to the new addition. They began to feel a little left out as the grandfather spent a great deal of time with Kodi and Pete who really seem to enjoy being in the, limelight, with an older person.

One day they took him to task, "Grandpa, why are you always doing what they wish to do. You don't pay any attention to us anymore!"

He then had to explain, "You have always been living here and have always had the best. They have come here only for a short holiday. As you are my grandchildren they are also the same. You are cousins, the same family and I have never seen them before. Don't you like them, too?"

"Yes, but I guess it's very hard to share you with them. "He then gave them a hug and they ran away to look for their new-found friends, who they now saw in a different light. Their mother had aso had to do the explaining for them to get a clearer picture. At first they were afraid to ask Pete for any help or to teach them something, until one day they decided to play basket –ball together. Pete gave them an opportunity to win whenever he could pretend. They weren't easily fooled and he realised that sometimes they could run faster than him.

CHAPTER 36

GENOVA

Gino's sister Marian was well-versed in the History of Italy. So she was the one who took them around the city and to tell them, all about Genova. Kodi was very keen on everything involved with History and Art. She was looking forward to discovering this city and it's surroundings.

Genova is the captital of Genova Province and the Liguria region in North Western Italy. It has a population of more than 2,200,000 and is located about 120Kms. south of Milan on the gulf of Genova, The Northern portion of the Mediterranean's Ligurain Sea. The harbour is, very busy because it is the most important seaport and one of the largest in Europe. The facilities of the port are used by ships and yachts all the year round. It is a port of call of passenger ships and car ferries that sail on both fixed and special schedules. So really if anyone wished to come in or escape from this area they would have no problems, at all especially from April to the end of October.

The climate is rather pleasant. It was a mixture of Continental climate with the influence of the Mediterranean Coast. It's average temperature is about 28° in Summer and no lower than 5° in Winter. The city is built up from the port area into the surrounding hills.

"I would like to live here, what about you Pete? We don't have to go very far away to ski in winter and we have the beach whenever we wish. Although I like winter I think it is too long in Canada." said Kodi.

"Well, maybe but what about my friends. Yes, I know we have a great deal of comforts here. Grandpa's house is enormous and is well situated. Do you know that the house is situated at the height of 115m. This is an exclusive area. Aren't they lucky to have their private beach and an area for their boat? I must tell my friends about their boat. Do you know that it is 35.95m long, it had 6 rooms tastefully decorated with all the comforts one could expect on a boat. The deck had lounge chairs and tables, with a wooden and brass railing all around it. The polished brass knobs shone in the sun. Most of the yacht was made up of the top most quality material..

"The economy, I was told was dominated by the activities of the port which was conveniently connected by rail, air and highway transportation systems that service the shipping industry. That was how the Felini economy, had grown so fast. Most of the jobs in the family, were involved with the sea and it's manufacures. Genova being the leading passenger port of the Mediterranean. In addition to shipping, iron and steel production and the manufactures of such diverse products as textile, munitions, paper products, locomotives and aircraft supplies, helped strengthen their economy. Their level of living was a great deal higher than the other provinces.

Kodi loved visiting Palaces. Since Genova is well-known for its medieval, Renaissance and Baroque palaces, she got to see a number of them. She greatly admired the, Ducal Palace, built in 1291 and the

16th century, The Dotia Tursi Palace, which is now being used as the City Hall. They visited The Cathedral of San Lorenzo –10th century and the churches of San Ambrogio and The Annunciaton which are examples of Baroque arquitecture. The also visited the Bianco Palce and the Rosso Place museums.

"I'm sorry, you would have to tell me that, I've always been very bad with History, "she pretended not to know any, which wasn't true.

"Well Doria, Christopher Columbus and Nicoli Paginni."

"Good for you, darling. I think I've had enough let's go back to the house." When they returned they has a shower and went down for lunch.

"We were very lucky to command a great view from the house, so there was not a boring moment. I felt that it was a great privilege to be here. It was something I had not dreamed of, so I wasn't surprised that the children were having a whale of a time.

I am sure the grandparents would have to take a holiday, after we leave as both the kids took turns in making them work overtime. In the mornings, they were invited down to the kitchen to help prepare the menu with the help of the grandmother and the cooks. Pete considered cooking, one of his hobbies. No doubt he was the main attraction there as he didn't hesitate to talk to everyone, to explain how to make some dishes. One day he actually cooked a meal for everyone, which they found delectable. No doubt the grandmother had to keep mum that she helped with the ingredients, as he was pretty ignorant of any of them. It was an extra special sauce with fish.

He was compensated when, "This is one of the most delicious dishes I have ever tasted." Said Tino and everyone agreed with him.

Many of hem took a second helping. Something about it that made Melani suspicious that her son was in the kitchen as it was laid out, the way he generally did. Do I know who the special cook you have employed for the day? "She asked.

"Well you won't believe it, but Pete made it!" said the grandma.

"In that case we have to sack the cook and get her replaced by Pete, no doubt!" Everyone agreed.

Pete was not abashed at all. He was pleased that they enjoyed it. "If that's the case grandpa, get your wallet ready. The salary of the cook will be twice as high as what you pay at the moment. Is that a deal?" They were all in splits.

"The job is yours. Let's sign the agreement, right now, before you change your mind." After everyone stopped laughing, he said, "Mum, I am taking cooking lessons from Grandma and the cooks."

Of course, Mama Fellini you, better keep him out of the kitchen if you don't want to get ruined. He has an appetite to make up for the rest of the family.

One day he told his grandmother, "I think you should convince mum to cook like you. You should ask her down to the kitchen!"

"No," said the grandmother. "She is rather tired. Didn't you tell me she works very hard and has hardly time for herself. You know it isn't easy to both study and take care of the house even if you say you give her a hand. What I have decided to do is, we are going to give her a present. Now don't you go and tell her about it. We have a special old book on recipes. It has come down to me from my grandmother. I have decided to make a copy for her and together with a number of ingredients. You must help me pack it up for her. Most of the recipes aren't difficult to follow. Your mother is a very smart lady. Now don't forget to teach her what you have been learning in the kitchen with me. It's important to remember some of the little secrets of the history of the Fellini cooks.

No doubt we'll get her to the kitchen when she is more relaxed, don't you think so?"

"Grandma, you are so very thoughtful! "With that he gave her a hug.

FELLINI FAMILY

The Fellini family had lived in Genova for generations and were well-known and respected by everyone around. We loved our children very dearly and always wanted them to live here and carry on with the family business. But Tino was a restless boy and loved travelling a great deal.

One day after his arrival home, after having spent his summer holidays in Toronto, he surprised us by saying, "I am now on holiday so I am going to enjoy these last few days as much as possible!"

"What do you mean?" asked his father quite taken aback.

"I am sorry to give you this news, you are not going to like it, but I have decided to leave Genova permanently and live in Canada."

"This of course completely upset both my wife and I, that's putting it mildly! It took us some time to get used to the idea. Especially my Angela, she was very upset, she couldn't accept the idea of his leaving the family, just like that. Fortunately we had the consolation that Gino was with us and that he would one day take over the reigns. Knowing fully well that I would get old some time we were keen on getting Gino to have more responsibility in the company here. He was a very hard worker and we could count on him for everything.

So we were really very happy when we discovered that he was going out with one of our neighbours' daughter that belonged to one of the oldest generations in Genova. Both our families did a great deal of business together. This would be a good union for both the families!" We thought.

"Grandpa!" said Pete as he burst, into the room. "Let's go to the somewhere special, you promised yesterday? Both Kodi and I are are ready."

With that he dragged his grandfather away, so that he could talk to him away from the presence of his mother.

"I am sorry Melani, we could continue this another time, I promised to take them out for the day."

"Don't worry, I know how excited they are to have someone like you, who is patient and loving. Both of them are affectionate children so they forget their manners, sometimes."

Turning to Pete, she said, "You can't just come in here like that and interrupt a conversation. It's very rude!" But she let him off with a loving tap on his back.

"I am sorry mum, but we won't have grandpa with us for a long time. Time is flying so fast, so we have to take advantage and spend as much time as possible with him. I hope you don't mind." He left with that naughty look on his face.

"Come on, go ahead."

She then turned away and decided to look for the rest of the Fellini home. This was a huge mansion, with about 12 rooms. They had eight bedrooms. Four of them had en-suite baths with a jacuzzi. They were all spacious and tastefully decorated. There were statues in the bath. Each held a plant. All the bedrooms had huge French windows with a terrace.

This was filled with exotic plants covered with the most colourful flowers. From here you commanded a view of the whole bay. Every window was a picture –window. If you didn't have the sea, you had the cliffs or the hills.

We had been given a very cosy room. Everything in pale blue and white. It overlooked the cliffs. On walking out to the terrace you could hear the lapping and lashing of the waves against the rocks. I could just stay there for hours, feasting on this delightful vision. Gio didn't quite care for the sea, unlike me. What surprised me more was that he loved swimming in the sea but something kept him away from it. Little did I know that it always reminded him of his home.

Numerous seagulls went gliding by, now and again they would go swooping swiftly into the sea, usually coming out with a prize. For me, being here, there was not a moment of boredom. I just loved every minute. Never ever felt so relaxed in my life.

"Why didn't Gio bring us here, earlier? "She has been asking herself a number of times. Too bad Pete interrupted our conversation! What would drag someone away from this exotic place with all the comforts and such loving parents? I knew that it had nothing to do with his parents nor his immediate family. It was clearly seen that they loved each other very dearly.

Often I'd ask myself, "Why 'Why?" But everytime we broached the subject about going to Italy, something would crop up. Doubtless to say he loved his job. He was happy designing a house or a swimming pool. Inspite of having a number of workers under his charge, often he'd go down on his knees or haunches to explain how the work should be done by doing it himself. They respected him greatly but knew that he was a hard task-master who not only demanded of them, but did the best he could. I couldn't complain because he treated me like a queen. We were very happy together. I couldn't ask for more. We were just a great family with normal everyday problems. "She reminisced –

Across from the house, on the opposite side, the sea turned into the bay which formed a natural harbour. This area had been divided into various sections, in a very organised manner.

On one side you see the fishing boats where there was a lot of activity going on in the mornings and in the late evenings The fisherman were early birds and would set sail long before sunrise. In the evenings they would be seen cleaning their boats, clearing seaweeds or tiny remnants of fish or debri from the sea.

On the Northern side was the Nautic Club where numerous luxury, pleasure boats and yachts, were moored to their respective anchors according to their size. You could see the boats moving with the currents, keeping in rhythm with the slight, early morning breeze that kept blowing. Further away in the horizon a couple of Luxury Liners could be seen cruising around the coasts of Italy and the rest of of the Mediterranean. It was not surprising to find this place very busy with many tourists.

That evening both Kodi and Pete came home after they had spent a long day our with their cousins, Elia and Bruno, their grandfather and their uncle Tino. They enjoyed being with their cousins who on occasions were a bit put out as Pete seemed to patronize their grandfather and often gave them little opportunity to make a choice about what they were doing.

The first couple of days they used to complain to their parents.

"Mum we don't get an opportunity to do what we want. Grandpa only listens to Pete and Kodi. He does whatever they want, not even giving us an opportunity!" complained Bruno

"Well, don't forget they are here only for a short time. You have always been with grandpa and he has always given you all his attention, so please don't complain. They are equally his grandchildren as you are. Come on, go and enjoy yourself. I see Pete showing you many little things, you didn't know about until his arrival here. You are always telling me that Pete did this and that for you. Now go on and enjoy yourself, while your cousins are here with you. They are both nice children."

Marian got rid of them like this.

The next day, "Mum, how would you like the idea of sailing along the coast line? You find the sea enticing so I don't have to tell you how exciting a trip around, could be." commented Pete in a very persuasive voice.

"Yes, that would be an excellent idea. Did your grandfather suggest it, or are you asking me to you talk to papa about it." She asked.

"This would be very relaxing for the two of you." he continued, "You have both worked a great deal the whole year round. Now is the time to take advantage and make the most of it!"

She realised that he was right! This idea was very tempting. She wanted Gio to get involved with the children more than he had been doing since their arrival. It seemed to be quite satisfied that his father had taken over the children.

After she had spoken to Gio he said,"Well, don't worry I'll talk to them!" He had hardly stopped talking when his children came in.

"So there you are dad. You seem to have forgotten us. Well we think it's time for us to do a family thing – altogether, not just grandfather and us, but everyone. Let's prepare a huge picnic basket, with loads of sandwiches, cool drinks and games, for tomorrow. Grandpa is prepared to take us in his boat. There's enough room for all of us.

Turning to his mom he said, "Mom, what a luxurious boat Grandpa has! I have never seen something like that. At least I have never ever got that close to seeing one and being inside. It is 35.40mts. long. It has a beautiful lounge to relax. There's a great collection of music, many table games. He showed us around, let both of us try steering the boat and gave us some Blackmagic chocolates. He had them in a cabinet on board. They just melted in the mouth as we ate them. We also had some cool drinks there. The whole scenery was breath-taking and when the sun began to get too strong we decided to leave the deck although there is a covered area that protected us from the intense sun., where we played a chess game and guess who won, none other than I – Junior Fellini beat Grandpa Fellini," he said filled with pride

As for Kodi she continued on deck reading a book. He has a mini library in there. Look at her, she's completely toasted, so am I" He said pointing out to Kodi. The next day they arranged for all the family to go on this little cruise.

The two of them soon disappeared, "I guess they are planning something and I wasn't supposed to be included", thought Melani as she smiled.

This trip should help take away the unpleasantness she had been feeling since talking to her father-in law. It seems as if something always came in the way to stop her from knowing the real reason why Gio hadn't brought them to Genoa before.

"I must get this out of my system by clarifying this with Gio tonight." She thought to herself That night she decided to stay awake as late as possible. It was so much fun listening to all the anecdotes the family had to tell each other. It reached a point when she found it rather tiring to have to concentrate in Italian, so much. She just had a spattering idea of it. At first Gio tried to translate all he could, but she realised that it was very difficult to continue breaking up the conversation, until such time as she told him, "Don't bother translating as I quite understand the idea, "which was far from the truth.

And even when they spoke in English she found it hard to understand as the accent was completely different. It was well past her sleeping time, so she couldn't help but call it a day and went to bed, leaving the rest who continued talking late into the night. Melani generally felt sleepy and retired earlier than the others. She was an early bird.

"I knew the feeling of being with the family and didn't grudge him any of those treasured moments because these were little luxuries of life to be treasured. I could see it meant a lot to him as I always had a similar experience everytime I went to visit my family. "

She woke up the next day revitalized and completely forgot the negative thoughts that she had been feeling the day before. She was now all fired up, for the cruise. Loving nature as much as she did, she was looking forward to sailing around the coastline, as much as her children. She wore a great big hat to protect her face and wore a pale green loose dress over her bikini. Her sandals were of the same colour with little flowers on it.

Gio seemed to have been injected with a good dose of positive attitude that brought that lustre back into his life. This was the second week. For once I never ever heard him talk about his job. He acquired a beautiful tan and really looked dashing. Many an eye turned towards him when he passed by women but he seemed oblivious to all of it. I could see that both the children and him seemed to be getting on well. He was pointing out places and even taking numerous photographs of them. Of and on he would switch that Video on me and the rest of the family.

Marian, his sister had that gypsy-look magnetism. Dark eyes and dark hair with slanting eyes more expressive with gestures than with words. I was told that she looked like her grandmother Geraldina. At first she had suspicion written all over her face the few times we ever got to be together. Of course she made sure never to be alone in my presence. She gave me the impression that she was not receptive to foreigners especially having someone so close to the family. I wonder if she even mistakenly, suspected that I was a fortune hunter.

Little did she know that I had no idea what-so-ever about the financial situation of this family, before coming here. Au contrar! Gino hardly ever spoke about his family. And I never tried to find out because every time I casually spoke about visiting Italy he conveniently evaded the subject.

That day I was determined to cut the distance that divided us Marian and I. This was the only opportunity, I got to get near enough to her. I suspected she didn't quite take to me at first. We had hardly exchanged a couple of words during the two weeks we spent together. So I decided to show her that I was no outsider but part of the family and there was no way I was going to accept being treated that way.

Earlier I had noticed from the balcony, before we left for the cruise, the dress she was wearing, so I looked around for something to go with it. "Voila!" I had it. Moments later, when we were on the boat, I managed to bring a smile on her face when I stuck a beautiful turquoise hat on her head that matched her off-shoulder dress. "Come on, look at yourself in the mirror, I think it suits you beautifully." I could see approval written all over her face.

"I hope you don't mind but this hat suits your dress", she said, as she replaced the one she had on.

"Oh thank you!" She said with a surprise. "I really love it!"

That did the trick. She broke into a broad smile.

I soon discovered that besides other traits she was also a bit shy but by the end of this trip we managed to unfold the curtain that seemed to divide us. She was more of an observer and a person of few words. We both seemed to be curious about each other. And I could clearly see that she wanted to find out why her brother had married out of the community and so I was perfectly aware of being under constant scrutiny, in her presence.

At first it was quite disconcerting, but I soon decided that I had a choice to either ignore her or get to know her. And Voila! The latter led me to discover that she was just worried about her brother and wanted to know all about his family and just maybe had been under the mistaken impression that I was keeping him away from them.

This was the golden opportunity I got. Since she began to open towards me, I thought that it was time I did some clarifying for her and for myself. Melani told her how she got to meet Gio. "Why didn't you all come to our wedding?" she asked.

"Well papa was a bit ill at that time so neither of us wanted to leave him back. But we were expecting you to visit us and we were very hurt when you didn't."

Well she didn't know why Gio didn't want to, but she wanted to cover up for him so she said, "I don't know whether your father is a workaholic or not but Gio is one. Even if he is ill he goes to work. "

She decided that this was the opportunity she had been looking forward to.

"Besides, I have a strong feeling that something must have happened here for his not really wanting to come here. Often I tried to convince him to pay all of you a visit but he always evaded the situation, with an excuse."

"Marianne, maybe you could explain why. Gio is a wonderful person and I hope you don't mind my asking you this. I know it's a bit delicate for me but I feel it's very important. First of all, I would like to know why your brother never wanted to bring us to Genova. I asked him many times and so did the children but he always had an excuse for not coming. I know he is a wonderful person and he loves us very much. He clearly loves all of you too, so why would he do such a thing. He is enjoying every moment here so what really is the problem? Often when I used to mention Genova, a shadow of sadness reflected on his face and he used to become very, very sad. But now he is quite relaxed. I guess with the years situations change."

"Well, I think Gino should have explained this to you. But if he didn't it is because it hurts him very much to do so. He was just 24, maybe a couple of years before he met you. I think he lost his head when he fell in love with a girl named Sofia, who lived in that mansion that is not far away from us. She pointed out to the direction of her house.

Both our families were very pleased and were expecting them to get married. They were inseparable and finally decided to get engaged. My parents were very happy, but frankly speaking, I thought that she was a spoilt bitch. I didn't care for her, very much. To me she was as shallow can be. She had everything a man would look for! Beauty, Intelligence and of course the money. Not that Gio really cared about her money. She was slim and tall 5ft 8, black, sparkling eyes and long black hair. Yes, she had very sharp features and attracted many men. They had actually fixed a date for the marriage but three months before they went to a friend's party and there ......"

At that moment, Gio came towards them with the camera, "what are the two of you doing here, stuck in this corner. Marian, you can do that when you are in the house."

With that he dragged Melani, "You are missing this rugged beauty that is all around us! You were the one to convince me to come, and then you go and hide yourself."

Although I was terribly disappointed, his exuberance caught up with me.

"I am sorry Marian, "as she turned and walked towards what Gio was pointing out to.

I knew that from that day onwards Marian would consider me differently. I was satisfied to feel that we had broken the ice. No I wasn't going to destroy these relaxing moments Gio was enjoying. He had specially had a tough year. Besides whatever had happened, was in his past and had nothing to do with me. He was a faithful husband and a great father. What more should I ask for. I guess he must have felt that his past had nothing to do with me.

That outing was indeed just wonderful for the whole family. Melani discovered that her in-laws were far from the people she had thought them to be. Fortunately, they had no idea of the harsh feelings she had harboured against them. They clearly showed how much they enjoyed having them in the house. The mother got the best food prepared by personally attending to the cooking.

"Mother hasn't been in the kitchen except to supervise, for quite some time. So you can be sure that she wants to give all of you the very best. Everyday she personally makes something, something that Gio used to enjoy very specially. It makes me happy to see her looking so radiant with happiness. Yes, we all missed Gio and wondered why he didn't bother to visit us all these years. We used to think that his wife had been responsible for his behaviour. But now that we have met you and the family we are very happy." Said Marian.

CHAPTER 38

MARIO

*I*t was vacation time for Mario, too. This year he decided that he wasn't going to travel. He had enough for the year travelling not only for the company but also for the family. He had a head for business and although he wasn't supposed to be working directly for the family business, he gave a hand when necessary, especially when it came to dealing with important customers from abroad. So it was a pretty taxing year for him.

The company he was working for was flourishing and that was why they had to build this new factory. They were one of the biggest chemical companies in Italy and exported to many European countries. Counterelli Chemicals had a big market in the East and sold a great variety of their products. For the past three years they began diversifying. They not only bought raw material – coal from the States which they refined and extracted all kinds of products but were also into the construction of new urbanizations and the building of car parts.

There were days when he hardly came home for a meal. Grabbing a snack here and there or going to a restaurant, near the company – so that they could continue discussing business. It was always that machine isn't working, the material hasn't arrived on time workers were behind schedule … quite a chain of events! What with the company having to open a new factory. So late nights with hardly four hours of sleep became the trend during the last six months and it began to take a toll on him. One day his boss told him, "I want you out of here as soon as we have all the new computers installed. The adaptation to new technology, involved a great deal of changes. That should take about three days. I will get some of the boys to help you."

When he felt that everything he had organized was running smoothly, he decided to take his well-deserved vacations. During this period he had lost a great deal of weight.

CHAPTER 39

THE SHOCK

ario was an early riser. He enjoyed riding his horse along the sea-shore, going for long walks and most often ended up having a swim. It was on one of these occasions that he suddenly caught sight of this figure that drew his attention. He thought it was unusual to see a woman alone, in the early hours of the morning. Not wanting to disturb her, he continued on his horse. But the next day she was seen again. He soon discovered that she was regularly seen at about the same hour every day.

It was Wednesday the 10th of August, the sun hadn't risen as yet. The sky was a mixture of splashes of blue and pink and there was a cool breeze blowing. He stopped enchanted when he saw her again, to watch her antics in the water and along the beach. She kept running with the waves as they receded, to collect shells. Sometimes she was seen chasing little crabs which usually got the better of her. He went a little closer but kept a distance as he didn't want to frighten her away. She looked so fragile, so nymph-like and carefree. He sort of felt that he was infringing on her privacy so he walked away.

The next day he decided to hide behind a rock from where he could command a clear view of her "Lo and behold," he said to himself, "I have seen this lady before!" So he got out of his hiding place and pretended to walk by her uninterestedly. He was no more than a few feet away when he realised that she was none other than Melani, who he had met in Virgina two years ago.

He froze, his life had taken a complete change after having met her. He lost interest in women and to his friends surprise he left their parties earlier than usual. He knew he was smitten by her and dreamed of seeing her again. Something about her had captured his attentions unlike most of his lady friends. On his return from Virginia he seemed a changed person. Every woman he went out with didn't last because his feelings for them didn't go beyond being platonic because this lady had enraptured him so greatly that he found it hard to maintain a close relationship with any other woman. This surely had many tongues wagging.

His mother was a little upset to see this change as she was looking forward to his settling down to having a family, but reframed from questioning him. If there's anything I am sure he will tell me in good time.

Now his excitement knew no bounds as he took another look at her again to make sure he wasn't dreaming. It was quite clear that she was unaware of the reaction she was causing …. She had not changed a day. His heart began to pound, each time louder but he decided to wait. He returned home a very cheerful person.

"What makes you so light-hearted today? I haven't heard you whistle or sing for such a long time," his mother asked looking at him suspiciously.

"Oh, I am just happy today. Is breakfast ready?" That day he had a sumptuous meal. For the next couple of days his mother noticed him spending more time on the terrace or looking out to sea.

"Why aren't you going out for your daily ride?" she asked.

"Oh, I just feel like enjoying the fresh air from here, for a change." Often she'd be talking to him and he wouldn't hear her. She would catch him lost in thought, instead of reading the magazine he had in his hands. These were some of the tell-tale signs that said a great change was taking over her son. She decided to observe him and was rewarded. Yes, the next day she discovered the object of his attention.

"Who is this person, I've never seen her before", she asked herself.

Melani decided to go to the very end of the beach where she saw those big boulders used as breakers to prevent the sea from carrying away the sand. I am going to climb up there and wait for sunrise.

She carefully walked around until she found a way of climbing up to the huge tall rock which was flat at the top. The going up was hard but being agile, she climbed up carefully. Some parts were pretty slippery, others were rugged and pointed so she sometimes had to go on her fours. She knew if she slipped she would end up in the deep waters that surrounded her. When she finally reached the top she sat down and waited. As soon as the pale pink streaks of light slowly began to break through the fine morning mist, she closed her eyes and said a wee prayer.

"Thank you Lord for giving me this priceless joy!"

She slowly opened her eyes as she felt the warm streaks of sunlight caress her, but was startled when she sensed a shadow that prevented the sun from shining fully on her face. So she turned.

"I am sorry if I startled you, but this is a wonderful surprise! I have been watching you for the past couple of days and today I knew I wasn't mistaken about you …. You are that lovely lady, I had met at the party at Ryan's place in Virginia. I couldn't help but come nearer to you for two reasons. At first, I was nervous about you getting up here all by yourself. You must know it is very dangerous. Secondly, I couldn't avoid speaking to you. Aren't you Melani? I could never forget you, as I have you engraved in my brain and had promised myself that I was going to see you again. You never answered my letters. I got your address from Ryan.

Yes, this was Mario of course. All those memories that was indelible, were brought to mind, all in the twinkling of an eye. As this fleeting thought crossed her mind, she answered softly. "Yes, how are you? What a nice surprise to see you!"

Now it was her turn to blush, yes she remembered him, this was her prince-charming, at that time …the person who had changed her otherwise drab life, even if were just for a short while.

With his arms stretched out, he enveloped her unconsciously the Italian way and gave her a hug. He nearly threw her off her feet, just missed falling into the sea together. For a moment they seemed to have forgotten time until reality brought her back to earth and she carefully pushed him aside.

He added, "Please forgive me, I got carried away with those pent-up feelings! You have no idea how much I have been looking forward to seeing you again. Your face haunted me for the past two years. I got no more than a sentence or two about you, everytime I tried to pry out some information from your sister. So you finally decided to come to Italy. Is your family with you?"

"Yes, my husband and my two children are here. We are living in The Fellini house, I guess you must know them!

"She spoke as a shiver ran through her body.

"Are you cold? Let me wrap this towel around you, "he said in a voice so filled with emotion, that she was spell-bound for a moment.

"No!" she said softly, as she kept trying to find her voice. "It's just the early morning chill besides I am a little wet, too."

He wrapped the towel around her. He tried to shake himself. Come back to reality ….

I've waited all this time …. I must be more careful. I shouldn't display my feelings in such an outrageous manner. After all she is a married woman! He thought desperately as truth hit home. No doubt she wouldn't be here if she wasn't still married.

Melani didn't seem to enjoy this torture of standing so near him. No words were spoken but realized how transparent she was and tried to hide her confusion with difficulty. There was something that seemed to hold them otherwise why would destiny bring them together again. These thoughts floated past her.

Mario had hoped that one day he would meet her again. He wanted her but knew that she the kind of steadfast person who loved her family and that nothing would shake her, if not she would have replied to his letters or given him a call. But something tells me that I am going to get her. I know she is forbidden fruit, but all the more I want her.

These past two years only helped to strengthen his feelings toward her when he discovered that nobody could take her place.

"These things don't happen to people like me … am I crazy? He constantly asked himself.

"Do you still wok for the same company or has your father decided that you had to take over the reigns? You must be married now? Do you have any children? "She was curious to know what he had done with his life. He was dashing as ever though a bit too slim and was sure that someone must have captured his heart.

"Eh, one question at a time. Now let me see … the most important to me is.. No, I am not married, nobody seems to like me. Do you? "He asked teasingly as his eyes seriously searched hers, anxiously waiting for a response.

She brushed him aside by ignoring his question, not before turning completely red. She gave a nervous laugh. Why does this man so disconcert me?

"A penny for your thoughts! I am still here and you are far away. I'd give anything to take a trip into the depths of that little head of yours, to know exactly what's going on in there. My intuitive feelings tell me something, but I may be wrong."

"Oh, it's late I better run. I am sure the family must be up. It was nice to see you again!" she said agitated. He held out his and as her hands wrapped around his, he gave her a caressing squeeze that sent those tiny needles of excitement running through her whole body that she shivered for the second time. "I must go!" As she remembered to return his towel.

"I'd say so long because I am sure we are going to see each other gain. How long are you going to be here as I would like to invite

Giovani and his family, to my place. We know each other very well. We used to go out a lot together when we were younger. He had a great deal of problems here, due to no fault of his own. I am sure he must have overcome them after all these years."

The comment about Gio worried her but she realised it wasn't appropriate to discuss that situation with him! With a wave of her hand, she hurriedly walked away.

CHAPTER 40

THE MARKET

When she returned to the house she rushed directly to the shower before anyone could discover her confusion. Not seeing anyone around she realised that they must be in the dining room.

"You're late today, what delayed you?" enquired Gio.

"Well today I decided to face the challenge of going to the very top of those rocks, which I had been longing to do as I wanted to see the sunrise from there. It was breath-taking. I wish you were there too." She said as her face lit up.

"You shouldn't be going out there alone. Had you tripped or hurt yourself or what's more you could have fallen into the sea. It's very deep there. It would have been too late for us to do anything about it. So please be careful!" Gio admonished.

"Now how come you guys are up so early", she turned to look at her children.

"Guess what Mum, grandpa is taking us somewhere very special, today. It's going to be a surprise! So when we return we'll tell you all about it."

"Enjoy yourself! But don't drive Papa Fellini crazy." With a kiss they were out of the door.

Turning to Gio, she said, "Your father looks very relaxed and looks younger. It's all the trotting about that's doing the trick."

"Father seems to be enjoying himself a great deal. I am happy we did come, after all. This has been the best holiday I have ever had. What about you? I can see that the sea has brought some colour into that pale skin of yours. Wouldn't it be wonderful if we settled down here? Both my parents think that it would be a good idea if we did, he asked."

"Well that could be a bit difficult with the kids having to finish their education. Yes they seem to be having a great time here, but don't forget that everything is new to them and they feel important with all the attention they are receiving. Things are different during holiday-time. What about the language barrier? Unless there is an English School here. But you never know. We could get their feedback on that.

Both Kodi and Pete enjoyed their outings with the grandfather especially their trips to the wharf. The number of ships from different countries and the constant loading and unloading was something they had never seen before. They described everything they saw. One day they were taken on board one of the ships. Here the captain even gave them the opportunity of learning many things. They learnt the use of most of the buttons and actually got to navigate a couple of knots.

I wonder why Papa never brought us here before thought Pete. Just at that precise moment interrupting him as if Kodi had read his thoughts. "I know why Dad didn't bring us here before. I think he wanted to have lots of money, so that we could have loads of fun. Aren't you glad we are here? Do you think mum is having fun? She really deserves to have a good time and so does Dad.

Papa Fellini had no problems when it came to buying fish. He usually went to the same fisherman, in the auction centre who always gave him the best. They traditionally ate a lot of fish. Today was different, he wanted to take his grandchildren and test their capabilities at how to auction. He was proud of them, so he liked to show them off to everyone especially after the scandal that had wrongly involved his son Giovani.

It didn't take long for Pete to get involved as he very carefully observed the vendors and buyers who were trying not only get the best price but also the best quality. He convinced his grandfather to take him there on a regular basis. He didn't mind getting up very early but Kodi decided to stay in bed a little longer. One day he actually got caught up by the atmosphere that without batting an eye-lid he offered a price for a basket of fish that astounded everyone watching. They clapped their hands at the accuracy of the price. His grandfather couldn't help laughing. This drew the attention of the rest of the crowd standing nearby, who joined in this sudden uproar.

"It's yours!" said the fisherman. Surprised by their re-action, he blushed. To make matters worse he realised his mistake …. He didn't have any money on him. He looked helplessly at his grandfather who had already had his wallet out which he handed to Pete. That's your fish.

When they arrived home at first Gio was annoyed when he heard about what had happened he didn't want Pete to get away just in case he repeated it.

"Pete, you will have to return the money your grandfather gave you and it will be taken out of your pocket money. Pete turned red but was interrupted by his grandfather.

"How dare you scold my grandson. He is part of the family and pays for nothing while I am around. "He gave him a pat on the back.

"Come on, go and get ready for breakfast, I am sure everyone is waiting for us. "

At the breakfast table everyone congratulated him on his buy. But there was also a great deal of laughter as everyone joined Kodi who couldn't control herself.

DIVINCHI

Silvano also belonged to the same social level as us and they partied a lot together. But one fine day he invited someone who was unknown to most people. This boy Lino Divinchi came from Milan. He soon became the rave of the town. All the women folk, never stopped talking about him and literally threw themselves at his feet. Yes, he was dashing, tall, blue eyed but dark haired. But to me he seemed rather reckless. Yes, he seemed to splash money and drove the most expensive cars and caused quite an impression in town. He became the life of every party. No party was popular unless he was present. His numerous parties were becoming quite the social event and most women vyied to be his partner. He was seen driving around with different women in different cars. It was at one of these parties which was supposed to be a bit wild, that Silvan introduced both Gino to Sofia

Disrespectful to everyone he just didn't care about anyone's feelings. He approached Sofia and asked her to dance with him. He easily swept her off her feet. From that day on she had no eyes for anyone except for Lino She literally forgot that she was supposed to be getting married to Gino in a few months. Both the families were supposed to be very disappointed as they had planned to join their businesses and to work together. Since his arrival, he seemed to create an upheaval and you could see all these women hanging all over him. Gino was very badly effected. He just couldn't handle that situation and often came home drunk.

One month later he packed and left. It seemed as if he had disappeared into thin air. We were very upset. My mother got very ill and my father wasn't any better, until we got the news that he had joined his brother in Canada. I tried to bring them back together but Sofia had no eyes for anybody except for Lino.

CHAPTER 42

DISASTEROUS END

A couple of months later Sofia was found burnt in her bed. The first thing her parents did was to call the cops and openly accused Gino of being responsible for it.

"We have no doubt that this is the result of her jealous lover. Gino was supposed to marry her but when he discovered that she no longer cared for him, he swore he would kill her. We have proof of these words, he shouted out when he was found completely drunk at one of the parties. Besides Mario could also testify how wild he had turned."

CHAPTER 43

THE THREATS

oth Silvano and Lino testified that Gino turned violent when he discovered that his wedding plans had been blown. At one of the parties he was stone drunk that he swore revenge.

"I am not going to lose my fiancee' to someone who flirts with every girl and flaunts around with all his flashy cars. I know that Sofia is being drugged by him. I will make sure that he is never seen in this town ever again. Besides I know that Sofia still cares for me. I am going to wring his head. I will not let him destroy the life of my wife –to-be."

All this was heard publicly, during one of the parties. Gino had to face numerous supposed to be friends, who were bought by Lino. They all testified against him.

CHAPTER 44

GINO ESCAPES

Gino realises the ugly situation he was facing. He could clearly see that he had lost Sofia. He tried all he could to get her out of his head. So when his brother convinced him that it was better for him to disappear from the great depression, he was going through, he realised that there was no alternative, but to put an end to his misery. Two days before she was found burnt in her bed, he left for Toronto- Canada.

INVESTIGATION

*I*t was awfully embarrassing for Gino's family when they discovered that the entrance to their home was covered with sirens, and numerous cops, all over the place. They even entered the house and left no stones unturned--- meaning they actually took the house to pieces. It didn't take long before the cops were in our house questioning every single person in the house even all the workers in the house. individually. They did a thorough search, of the whole house although we everyone tried to explain to them that he had left for Canada. The cops didn't believe a word. Some of them had their pockets lined by Lino.

Sofia's parents insisted that he was seen in the house nearly every day. Lino Divinchy played the part of a devastated lover. He stayed constantly beside her parents. They testified that he rushed to to help when her parents gave him a call to say that Sofia was on fire. He showed them all the burns he had, had in many parts of his body.

During the interrogation he was all tears. He played the innocent lover who had lost his beloved. Both his parents and her parents joined forces and told the cops, "Don't spare any money, we want the culprit found, we know that this is the work of her Giovani her ex-lover. He was seen drunk in most of the bars and was heard saying that he would kill her. This of course was heard by numerous companions and supposed-to-be friends.

CHAPTER 46

THE DISCOVERY

ortunately all the cops weren't corrupt. After having involved Interpol they were able to verify that Gino had indeed left the country for Canada, a couple of days before this treacherous happening, had occurred. They discovered that the false stories that spread like wild fire about Gino's involvement with the death of Sofia.

They later discovered that Sofia's mother was also involved – she was having an affair with Lino who shame-facededly took advantage of every opportunity that came his way. She gave birth to her child when she was just sixteen. Both Mother and daughter were raving beauties.

At first sight it was apparent, she must have been drunk or drugged and could have been smoking in bed. She must have been smoking when she fell asleep, after having dropped the cigarette butt on the bed. The satin sheets caught fire and supposedly her satin nightee, too. The moment one of the maids smelt fire she had the presence of mind of first calling the firemen and the police and then ran to call her parents who were dead to the world. The firemen were there very shortly, but the servants of the house were already trying to put off the fire together. Altogether they, managed to stop the fire from spreading and her body was more than half burnt, but it was too late. But when the paramedics arrived, they rushed her to the hospital where they discovered that she was dead.

Gino's parent when questioned insisted on having the a thorough forensic investigation.

Yes, on searching Sofia's house, they did discover a couple of cigarette butts around the room on the floor. On re-examining they discovered that they couldn't have been smoked by the same person as they were of two different brands and on questioning all the guests who had attended a party the previous day they discovered that Sofia was completely drunk the night before as Lino was dancing with another women which he completely denied.

One of the under –cover cops managed to enter Lino's hotel room with an authorized request to investigate Lino. They discovered the packet of cigarettes of which a couple of them had been found in Sofia's bed that was stuck in one of the corners of her bed which had escaped the fire.

Besides the traces of drugs found in her body, was also found in Lino's room.

Another Investigator approached the Custom's officers wno were on duty the day Gino had left the country. Gino's passport that had been confiscated also justified that he had left two days before the incident took place.

Lino was taken into custody and was facing life imprisonment.

REPERCUSSIONS

Gino reached a point he couldn't handle the investigation, when he saw how much of suffering his parents had to face. Besides the death of Sofia caused a great impact on him. Taking his father's boat he sped across the open ocean after having downed more alcohol his body could hold. He crashed against the cliffs. The collective work of a number of four coast guards found his body beyond salvation. The whole town moaned his loss.

Melani, the children and his family were filled with grief. It had taken it's toll specially on the children.

All this made them reach the decision of living with their grandparents.

CHAPTER 48

THE AFTERMATH

Living in Genova brought Mario closer to Melani. Gino's family were very fond of him. He used to visit them often during the period that Gino lived in Genova.

They welcomed him as part of the family.

A year later, he decided to quit his job and promote the family business. His parents were overwhelmed to have their son back. He became a frequent visitor at Gino's house. The children soon began to get closer to him. They spent a lot of time together, practising water-sports.

They decided to get married and live a peaceful life ever-after.